## THE AUTHOR

Edward Frederic Benson was born at Wellington College, Berkshire, in 1867. He was one of an extraordinary family. His father Edward White Benson – first headmaster of Wellington – later became Chancellor of Lincoln Cathedral, Bishop of Truro and Archbishop of Canterbury. His mother, Mary Sidgwick, was described by Gladstone as 'the cleverest woman in Europe'. Two children died young but the other four, bachelors all, achieved distinction: Arthur Christopher as Master of Magdalene College, Cambridge, and a prolific author; Maggie as an amateur egyptologist; Robert Hugh as a Catholic priest and propagandist novelist; and Fred.

Like his brothers and sisters, Fred was a precocious scribbler. He was still a student at Cambridge when he published his first book, *Sketches from Marlborough*. While he was working as an archaeologist in Athens, his first novel *Dodo* (1893) was published to great success. Thereafter Benson devoted himself to writing, playing sports, watching birds and gadding about. He mixed with the best and brightest of his day: Margot Asquith, Marie Corelli, his mother's friend Ethel Smyth and many other notables found their eccentricities exposed in the shrewd, hilarious world of his fiction.

Around 1918, E. F. Benson moved to Rye, Sussex. He was inaugurated mayor of the town in 1934. There in his garden room, the collie Taffy beside him, Benson wrote many of his comical novels, his sentimental fiction, ghost stories, informal biographies and reminiscences – almost one hundred books in all. Ten days before his death on 29 February 1940, E. F. Benson delivered to his publishers a last autobiography, *Final Edition*.

The Hogarth Press also publishes *Mrs Ames, Paying Guests, Secret Lives, As We Are, As We Were, Dodo – An Omnibus, The Freaks of Mayfair* and *The Luck of the Vails*.

# THE BLOTTING BOOK

## E. F. Benson

*New Introduction by*
*Stephen Knight*

x

THE HOGARTH PRESS
LONDON

Published in 1987 by
The Hogarth Press
Chatto & Windus Ltd
30 Bedford Square, London WCIB 3RP

First published in Great Britain by William Heinemann 1908
Hogarth edition offset from original Heinemann edition
Copyright the Executors of the Estate of the Revd K. S. P. McDowall
Introduction copyright © Stephen Knight 1987

*Second impression 1988*

British Library Cataloguing in Publication Data

BENSON, E.F.
THE BLOTTING BOOK.
I. TITLE
823'.8[F]   PR6003.E66

ISBN 0 7012 0763 9

Printed in Great Britain by
Cox & Wyman Ltd
Reading, Berkshire

# INTRODUCTION

After producing in 1901 that composed and suspenseful book *The Luck of the Vails*, E. F. Benson returned to his normal pattern – tales of the macabre, disarming society novels, tomes on sport and history. Then in 1908 he published a classic study of concealed crime, *The Blotting Book*. Those were his only criminographical ventures. Few other writers of thrillers have refused to return to that popular and lucrative genre once they have mastered it. Only Wilkie Collins, with *The Moonstone* and his chilling *The Woman in White*, has a pattern similar to Benson's, and he worked before crime fiction was fully established as genre or public success.

Of course, Benson, as a son of the Archbishop of Canterbury and a literary man about town, was rather above the forces of the publishing market, but he was not toying fashionably with the thriller – it had not yet become a relaxation for the literary elite. Rather, he seems to have been briefly swept on the flow tide of the crime novel, as it developed out of the widespread popularity of the short story mystery.

In 1907 Gaston Leroux's *La Mystère de la Chambre Jaune* was a *succès d'éstime* and *de scandale*; Austin Freeman's scientistic puzzles started at novel length with *The Red Thumb Mark* in the same year. These may have overtly persuaded Benson towards the form, but his work seems part of an international pattern: in 1908 Mary Roberts Rhinehart began, with her second novel *The Circular Staircase*, the first long career of a bestselling author of American tales of detection.

The short story and its techniques where fully established with leaders like Doyle and Hornung, brothers in law and illegality. The newly emerging novel form required new methods; it demanded a more sustained style of writing, with slower narrative development, fuller contextual setting and greater range of insight into character – those features might easily become mechanistic, but there had to be more of them. The novel also required, for real success, a much more manifold plot. Doyle claimed, with some reason, that his stories contained enough story for a full-length treatment, but few of his competitors could say the same and his own compression could at times conceal a threadbare plot development. To sustain mystery in the larger scope, the classic clue-puzzle programme of misdirection was needed, with false suspicions, bogus information, plot reversals and plain red herrings.

In *The Blotting Book*, Benson solved these problems of style and structure as if they contained no difficulties. Not all the ramifications of the golden age crime writers are present of course, but many are predicted. Agatha Miller was sixteen and just beginning to write fiction in 1908. Did the genteel bookish girl from Torquay, to become the nonpareil of crime writing, read Benson's tale of covert violence in Brighton? There are some striking resemblances between her launch vehicle, *The Murder of Roger Ackroyd*, and *The Blotting Book*.

Himself upper middle class, with a restless and slightly mischievous intelligence, Benson reconstructs from the start his own world and a sense of its perils. Effortless superiority reigns as the novel opens:

Mrs. Assheton's house in Sussex Square, Brighton, was appointed with that finish of smooth stateliness which robs stateliness of its formality, and conceals the amount of trouble and personal attention which has, originally in any case, been spent on the production of the smoothness.

Is he describing a style of life or a style of writing? Surely, both. The two continue their helical partnership up through the excellence of Mrs. Assheton's appointments, her deft and noiseless parlour-maids, the shine of her parquetry and all her surfaces, until the point, sharp and penetrating, is reached: "the moment when before dessert the cloth was withdrawn and showed a rosewood table that might have served for a mirror to Narcissus".

Narcissism may haunt his mother's world, but Morris

Assheton's problems are the opposite. He is too far committed in love and enmeshed in inheritance problems, bound to faithless trustees who intervene between him and the girl of his heart. As a result there appear flaws in his own glass. In the polished surface of his life style, rubescent with fine new car, motherly affections, gentlemanly leisure, there can also be seen the dark visage of violence. Morris cannot treat his love problems as a misunderstanding to be endured and outworn; a high-blooded nature seems to demand blood.

His youthful hyperbole is an elegant foil for the more torpid style of Mr. Taynton, solicitor to the family and trusted friend. Yet even here Benson suggests that all is not quite easy. What of the vignette where Mr. Taynton takes the nutcrackers and is "gravely exploding the shells of the nuts he had helped himself to"? The scene and the language both seem a little jarring. Taynton is a model bourgeois professional of a presumably vanished kind: he reads "as his custom was, a few collects and some short piece of the Bible to his servants before having his breakfast". And yet there seem uncertainties in his world, moments when his gaze is unduly attentive; and is his habit of losing at games to young men entirely innocent?

The shape of short story grown into novel is quite apparent. Benson makes do with few characters. In many ways *The Blotting Book* is a psychodrama among well-known people, looking forward to the methods of A. B. Cox, especially when he wrote as Francis Iles. Here there is no real detective; Superintendent Figgis thinks with his mouth open most of the time. The story sets itself out, and the mystery is revealed through the narrative's delicate approach to the characters' inner demons.

But the elements of a classic clue-puzzle are also present, time and place are as important as they would be to the Detection Club. And misdirections develop literary doubts just as disconcerting as the random suspicions of daily life. Is it important to establish the day on which Mills died, and is the newspaper in his pocket of moment or not? Did he really alight from the train at Falmer or only suggest that he would do so? What is the meaning of Martin, the former criminal? That stick, is it central, trivial or an unresolved matter? Should we remember the opening business about the will? Is it important to follow closely all of Taynton's epistolary activity? What is Mrs. Assheton actually doing when the story ignores her? How far is it to, and indeed from, the Templeton's house? Which of all these are red herrings?

The solution to the plot itself is not a sudden surprise, or should not be if you have paid attention and your copy has all the chapters. This is a shapely and convincing novel, not a game to tease the brain. The ending is both sad and fitting, given the forces that operate in this *haut bourgeois* world. The plot and the problem are not the whole novel. Benson does not merely pad out a puzzle with elegant settings and thoughtful insights into character *à la* Michael Innes. Like Collins in *The Woman in White*, and like the best of crime fiction, he moves into a richer register, that of the novel proper.

In large part that force is found through the quality of the settings. Not only in Mrs. Assheton's narcissistic ambience; mood and omen are found in all of Benson's scenes, impressionist moving towards expressionist. Morris's dream is well worth studying, both the first and the second time you read the novel; like Hammett's famous Flitcraft story, it synopsises not so much the action as the theme. When Taynton walks on the downs he imaginatively hears the cries of those who died in the Roman wars. History in this novel is human and painful, not the source of arid trickery it became in the detective story of later and more reductive years.

True, the subsequent and ingenious development of the form has its reflexive impact on Benson's early adventure; clues may seem too obvious now, misdirections might be ignored as too evidently amiss. The final statement by the judge could well, after decades of courtroom scenes, seem injudicious to a degree. But spirit remains strong in *The Blotting Book*.

And it is ultimately a blotting book itself, images of a leisured life style whose unconsidered relicts can be examined in reversed and so revealing form. Like his characters, Benson would no doubt demur at the imputation of such seriousness.

But then sheer talent like Benson's, in relaxed mode as in this book, can produce remarkable patterns of veracity and vitality, as the other game-playing early crime writers had shown, especially Doyle and Hornung. Like the ultimately vindicated Figgis, we may find depths of interest and even fragments of truth if we thoughtfully inspect *The Blotting Book*.

*Stephen Knight, Sydney 1986*

# The Blotting Book

## CHAPTER I

MRS. ASSHETON'S house in Sussex Square, Brighton, was appointed with that finish of smooth stateliness which robs stateliness of its formality, and conceals the amount of trouble and personal attention which has, originally in any case, been spent on the production of the smoothness. Everything moved with the regularity of the solar system, and, superior to that wild rush of heavy bodies through infinite ether, there was never the slightest fear of comets streaking their unconjectured way across the sky, or meteorites falling on unsuspicious picnicers. In Mrs. Assheton's

3

house, supreme over climatic conditions, nobody ever felt that rooms were either too hot or too cold, a pleasantly fresh yet comfortably warm atmosphere pervaded the place, meals were always punctual and her admirable Scotch cook never served up a dish which, whether plain or ornate, was not, in its way, perfectly prepared. A couple of deft and noiseless parlour-maids attended to and anticipated the wants of her guests, from the moment they entered her hospitable doors till when, on their leaving them, their coats were held for them in the most convenient possible manner for the easy insertion of the human arm, and the tails of their dinner-coats cunningly and unerringly tweaked from behind. In every way in fact the house was an example of perfect comfort; the softest carpets overlaid the floors, or, where the polished wood was left bare, the parquetry shone with a moonlike

radiance; the newest and most enter-
taining books (ready cut) stood on
the well-ordered shelves in the sitting-
room to beguile the leisure of the
studiously minded; the billiard table
was always speckless of dust, no tip
was ever missing from any cue, and
the cigarette boxes and match-stands
were always kept replenished. In
the dining-room the silver was resplen-
dent, until the moment when before
dessert the cloth was withdrawn,
and showed a rosewood table that
might have served for a mirror to
Narcissus.

Mrs. Assheton, until her only sur-
viving son Morris had come to live
with her some three months ago on
the completion of his four years
at Cambridge, had been alone, but
even when she was alone this ceremony of drawing the cloth and
putting on the dessert and wine had
never been omitted, though since she

never took either, it might seem to
be a wasted piece of routine on the
part of the two noiseless parlour-
maids. But she did not in the least
consider it so, for just as she always
dressed for dinner herself with the
same care and finish, whether she was
going to dine alone or whether, as to-
night, a guest or two was dining
with her, as an offering, so to speak,
on the altar of her own self-respect,
so also she required self-respect and
the formality that indicated it on
the part of those who ministered at
her table, and enjoyed such excellent wages. This pretty old-fashioned
custom had always been the rule
in her own home, and her husband
had always had it practised during
his life. And since then — his death
had occurred some twenty years ago —
nothing that she knew of had happened to make it less proper or
desirable. Kind of heart and warm

of soul though she was, she saw no
reason for letting these excellent qualities cover any slackness or breach of
observance in the social form of life
to which she had been accustomed.
There was no cause, because one was
kind and wise, to eat with badly
cleaned silver, unless the parlour-maid
whose office it was to clean it was
unwell.   In such a case, if the extra
work entailed by her illness would
throw too much on the shoulders
of the other servants, Mrs. Assheton
would willingly clean the silver herself, rather than that it should appear
dull and tarnished.   Her formalism,
such as it was, was perfectly simple
and sincere.   She would, without any
very poignant regret or sense of martyr-
dom, had her very comfortable income
been cut down to a tenth of what
it was, have gone to live in a four-
roomed cottage with one servant.   But
she would have left that four-roomed

cottage at once for even humbler surroundings had she found that her straitened circumstances did not permit her to keep it as speckless and *soignée* as was her present house in Sussex Square.

This achievement of having lived for nearly sixty years so decorously may perhaps be a somewhat finer performance than it sounds, but Mrs. Assheton brought as her contribution to life in general a far finer offering than that, for though she did not propose to change her ways and manner of life herself, she was notoriously sympathetic with the changed life of the younger generation, and in consequence had the confidence of young folk generally. At this moment she was enjoying the fruits of her liberal attitude in the volubility of her son Morris, who sat at the end of the table opposite to her. His volubility was at present concerned with his motor-car, in which he had arrived that afternoon.

"Darling mother," he was saying, "I really was frightened as to whether you would mind. I could n't help remembering how you received Mr. Taynton's proposal that you should go for a drive in his car. Don't you remember, Mr. Taynton? Mother's nose *did* go in the air. It's no use denying it. So I thought, perhaps, that she would n't like my having one. But I wanted it so dreadfully, and so I bought it without telling her, and drove down in it to-day, which is my birthday, so that she could n't be too severe."

Mr. Taynton, while Morris was speaking, had picked up the nutcrackers the boy had been using, and was gravely exploding the shells of the nuts he had helped himself to. So Morris cracked the next one with a loud bang between his white even teeth.

"Dear Morris," said his mother, "how foolish of you. Give Mr. Morris another nutcracker," she added to the parlour-maid.

"What's foolish?" asked he, cracking another.

"Oh Morris, your teeth," she said. "Do wait a moment. Yes, that's right. And how can you say that my nose went in the air? I'm sure Mr. Taynton will agree with me that that is really libellous. And as for your being afraid to tell me you had bought a motor-car yourself, why, that is sillier than cracking nuts with your teeth."

Mr. Taynton laughed a comfortable middle-aged laugh.

"Don't put the responsibility on me, Mrs. Assheton," he said. "As long as Morris's bank doesn't tell us that his account is overdrawn, he can do what he pleases. But if we are told that, then down comes the cartloads of bricks."

"Oh, you are a brick all right, Mr. Taynton," said the boy. "I could stand a cartload of you."

Mr. Taynton, like his laugh, was comfortable and middle-aged. Solicitors are supposed to be sharp-faced and fox-like, but his face was well-furnished and comely, and his rather bald head beamed with benevolence and dinner.

"My dear boy," he said, "and it is your birthday — I cannot honour either you or this wonderful port more properly than by drinking your health in it."

He began and finished his glass to the health he had so neatly proposed, and Morris laughed.

"Thank you very much," he said. "Mother, do send the port round. What an inhospitable woman!"

Mrs. Assheton rose.

"I will leave you to be more hospitable than me, then, dear," she said.

"Shall we go, Madge? Indeed, I am afraid you must, if you are to catch the train to Falmer."

Madge Templeton got up with her hostess, and the two men rose too. She had been sitting next Morris, and the boy looked at her eagerly.

"It's too bad, your having to go," he said. "But do you think I may come over to-morrow, in the afternoon some time, and see you and Lady Templeton?"

Madge paused a moment.

"I am so sorry," she said, "but we shall be away all day. We shan't be back till quite late."

"Oh, what a bore," said he, "and I leave again on Friday. Do let me come and see you off then."

But Mrs. Assheton interposed.

"No, dear," she said, "I am going to have five minutes' talk with Madge before she goes and we don't want you. Look after Mr. Taynton. I know he wants to talk to you and I want to talk to Madge."

Mr. Taynton, when the door had closed behind the ladies, sat down again with a rather obvious air of proposing to enjoy himself. It was quite true that he had a few pleasant things to say to Morris, it is also true that he immensely appreciated the wonderful port which glowed, ruby-like, in the nearly full decanter that lay to his hand. And, above all, he, with his busy life, occupied for the most part in innumerable small affairs, revelled in the sense of leisure and serene smoothness which permeated Mrs. Assheton's house. He was still a year or two short of sixty, and but for his very bald and shining head would have seemed younger, so fresh was he in complexion, so active, despite a certain reassuring corpulency, was he in his movements. But

when he dined quietly like this, at
Mrs. Assheton's, he would willingly have sacrificed the next five years
of his life if he could have been as-
sured on really reliable authority—
the authority for instance of the
Recording Angel—that in five years
time he would be able to sit quiet
and not work any more.  He wanted
very much to be able to take a pas-
sive instead of an active interest in
life, and this a few hundreds of pounds
a year in addition to his savings
would enable him to do.  He saw,
in fact, the goal arrived at which he
would be able to sit still and wait
with serenity and calmness for the
event which would certainly relieve
him of all further material anxieties.
His very active life, the activities of
which were so largely benevolent, had
at the expiration of fifty-eight years
a little tired him.  He coveted the
leisure which was so nearly his.

Morris lit a cigarette for himself, having previously passed the wine to Mr. Taynton.

"I hate port," he said, "but my mother tells me this is all right. It was laid down the year I was born by the way. You don't mind my smoking do you?"

This, to tell the truth, seemed almost sacrilegious to Mr. Taynton, for the idea that tobacco, especially the frivolous cigarette, should burn in a room where such port was being drunk was sheer crime against human and divine laws. But he could scarcely indicate to his host that he should not smoke in his own dining-room.

"No, my dear Morris," he said, "but really you almost shock me, when you prefer tobacco to this nectar, I assure you nectar. And the car, now, tell me more about the car."

Morris laughed.

"I'm so deeply thankful I have n't overdrawn," he said. "Oh, the car's a clipper. We came down from Haywards Heath the most gorgeous pace. I saw one policeman trying to take my number, but we raised such a dust, I don't think he can have been able to see it. It's such rot only going twenty miles an hour with a clear straight road ahead."

Mr. Taynton sighed, gently and not unhappily.

"Yes, yes, my dear boy, I so sympathise with you," he said. "Speed and violence is the proper attitude of youth, just as strength with a more measured pace is the proper gait for older folk. And that, I fancy is just what Mrs. Assheton felt. She would feel it to be as unnatural in you to care to drive with her in her very comfortable victoria as she would feel it to be unnatural in herself to wish to go in your lightning

speed motor.  And that reminds me.
As your trustee ——''

Coffee was brought in at this
moment, carried, not by one of the
discreet parlour-maids, but by a young
man-servant.  Mr. Taynton, with the
port still by him, refused it, but looked
rather curiously at the servant.
Morris however mixed himself a cup
in which cream, sugar, and coffee were
about equally mingled.

"A new servant of your mother's?"
he asked, when the man had left the
room.

"Oh no.  It's my man, Martin.
Awfully handy chap.  Cleans silver,
boots and the motor.  Drives it, too,
when I'll let him, which isn't very
often.  Chauffeurs are such rotters,
aren't they?  Regular chauffeurs I
mean.  They always make out that
something is wrong with the car, just
as dentists always find some hole in
your teeth, if you go to them.''

Mr. Taynton did not reply to these critical generalities but went back to what he had been saying when the entry of coffee interrupted him.

"As your mother said," he remarked, "I wanted to have a few words with you. You are twenty-two, are you not, to-day? Well, when I was young we considered anyone of twenty-two a boy still, but now I think young fellows grow up more quickly, and at twenty-two, you are a man nowadays, and I think it is time for you, since my trusteeship for you may end any day now, to take a rather more active interest in the state of your finances than you have hitherto done. I want you in fact, my dear fellow, to listen to me for five minutes while I state your position to you."

Morris indicated the port again, and Mr. Taynton refilled his glass.

"I have had twenty years of steward-ship for you," he went on, "and

before my stewardship comes to an
end, which it will do anyhow in three
years from now, and may come to an
end any day —— "

"Why, how is that?" asked Morris.

"If you marry, my dear boy. By
the terms of your father's will, your
marriage, provided it takes place with
your mother's consent, and after your
twenty-second birthday, puts you in
complete control and possession of
your fortune. Otherwise, as of course
you know, you come of age, legally
speaking, on your twenty-fifth birthday."

Morris lit another cigarette rather
impatiently.

"Yes, I knew I was a minor till I
was twenty-five," he said, "and I
suppose I have known that if I
married after the age of twenty-two,
I became a major, or whatever you
call it. But what then? Do let us
go and play billiards, I'll give you

twenty-five in a hundred, because I've been playing a lot lately, and I'll bet half a crown."

Mr. Taynton's fist gently tapped the table.

"Done," he said, "and we will play in five minutes. But I have something to say to you first. Your mother, as you know, enjoys the income of the bulk of your father's property for her lifetime. Outside that, he left this much smaller capital of which, as also of her money, my partner and I are trustees. The sum he left you was thirty thousand pounds. It is now rather over forty thousand pounds, since we have changed the investments from time to time, and always, I am glad to say, with satisfactory results. The value of her property has gone up also in a corresponding degree. That, however, does not concern you. But since you are now twenty-two, and your marriage would put the whole of this smaller sum into your hands, would it not be well for you to look through our books, to see for yourself the account we render of our stewardship?"

Morris laughed.

"But for what reason?" he asked. "You tell me that my portion has increased in value by ten thousand pounds. I am delighted to hear it. And I thank you very much. And as for ——"

He broke off short, and Mr. Taynton let a perceptible pause follow before he interrupted.

"As for the possibility of your marrying?" he suggested.

Morris gave him a quick, eager, glance.

"Yes, I think there is that possibility," he said. "I hope — I hope it is not far distant."

"My dear boy——" said the lawyer.

"Ah, not a word. I don't know——"

Morris pushed his chair back quickly, and stood up—his tall slim figure outlined against the sober red of the dining-room wall. A plume of black hair had escaped from his well-brushed head and hung over his forehead, and his sun-tanned vivid face looked extraordinarily handsome. His mother's clear-cut energetic features were there, with the glow and buoyancy of youth kindling them. Violent vitality was his also; his was the hot blood that could do any deed when the life-instinct commanded it. He looked like one of those who could give their body to be burned in the pursuit of an idea, or could as easily steal, or kill, provided only the deed was vitally done in the heat of his blood. Violence was clearly his mode of life: the motor had to go sixty miles an hour; he might be one of those who bathed in the Serpentine in mid-winter; he would clearly dance all night, and ride all day, and go on till he dropped in the pursuit of what he cared for. Mr. Taynton, looking at him as he stood smiling there, in his splendid health and vigour felt all this. He felt, too, that if Morris intended to be married to-morrow morning, matrimony would probably take place.

But Morris's pause, after he pushed his chair back and stood up, was only momentary.

"Good God, yes; I'm in love," he said. "And she probably thinks me a stupid barbarian, who likes only to drive golfballs and motor-cars. She — oh, it's hopeless. She would have let me come over to see them to-morrow otherwise."

He paused again.

"And now I've given the whole show away," he said.

Mr. Taynton made a comfortable sort of noise. It was compounded of laughter, sympathy, and comprehension.

"You gave it away long ago, my dear Morris," he said.

"You had guessed?" asked Morris, sitting down again with the same quickness and violence of movement, and putting both his elbows on the table.

"No, my dear boy, you had told me, as you have told everybody, without mentioning it. And I most heartily congratulate you. I never saw a more delightful girl. Professionally also, I feel bound to add that it seems to me a most proper alliance — heirs should always marry heiresses. It" — Mr. Taynton drank off the rest of his port — "it keeps properties together."

Hot blood again dictated to Morris: it seemed dreadful to him that any thought of money or of property could be mentioned in the same breath as that which he longed for. He rose again as abruptly and violently as he had sat down.

"Well, let 's play billiards," he said. "I—I don't think you understand a bit. You can't, in fact."

Mr. Taynton stroked the tablecloth for a moment with a plump white forefinger.

"Crabbed age and youth," he remarked. "But crabbed age makes an appeal to youth, if youth will kindly call to mind what crabbed age referred to some five minutes ago. In other words, will you, or will you not, Morris, spend a very dry three hours at my office, looking into the account of my stewardship? There was thirty thousand pounds, and there now is—or should we say 'are'— forty. It will take you not less than two hours, and not more than three. But since my stewardship may come to an end, as I said, any day, I should,

not for my own sake, but for yours,
wish you to see what we have done
for you, and — I own this would be a
certain private gratification to me —
to learn that you thought that the
trust your dear father reposed in us
was not misplaced."

There was something about these
simple words which touched Morris.
For the moment he became almost
businesslike. Mr. Taynton had been,
as he knew, a friend of his father's,
and, as he had said, he had been
steward of his own affairs for twenty
years. But that reflection banished
the businesslike view.

"Oh, but two hours is a fearful
time," he said. "You have told
me the facts, and they entirely satisfy
me. And I want to be out all day
to-morrow, as I am only here till the
day after. But I shall be down again
next week. Let us go into it all
then. Not that there is the slightest

use in going into anything. And when, Mr. Taynton, I become steward of my own affairs, you may be quite certain that I shall beg you to continue looking after them. Why you gained me ten thousand pounds in these twenty years — I wonder what there would have been to my credit now if I had looked after things myself. But since we are on the subject I should like just this once to assure you of my great gratitude to you, for all you have done. And I ask you, if you will, to look after my affairs in the future with the same completeness as you have always done. My father's will does not prevent that, does it?"

Mr. Taynton looked at the young fellow with affection.

"Dear Morris," he said gaily, "we lawyers and solicitors are always supposed to be sharks, but personally I am not such a shark as that. Are

you aware that I am paid £200 a year
for my stewardship, which you are
entitled to assume for yourself on
your marriage, though of course its
continuance in my hands is not forbidden in your father's will? You
are quite competent to look after
your affairs yourself; it is ridiculous
for you to continue to pay me this
sum. But I thank you from the bottom
of my heart for your confidence in me."

A very close observer might have
seen that behind Mr. Taynton's kind
gay eyes there was sitting a personality, so to speak, that, as his mouth
framed these words, was watching
Morris rather narrowly and anxiously.
But the moment Morris spoke this
silent secret watcher popped back
again out of sight.

"Well then I ask you as a personal
favour," said he, "to continue being
my steward. Why, it's good business
for me, is n't it? In twenty years you

make me ten thousand pounds, and I only pay you £200 a year for it. Please be kind, Mr. Taynton, and continue making me rich. Oh, I 'm a jolly hard-headed chap really; I know that it is to my advantage."

Mr. Taynton considered this a moment, playing with his wine glass. Then he looked up quickly.

"Yes, Morris, I will with pleasure do as you ask me," he said.

"Right oh. Thanks awfully. Do come and play billiards."

Morris was in amazing luck that night, and if, as he said, he had been playing a lot lately, the advantage of his practice was seen chiefly in the hideous certainty of his flukes, and the game (though he received twenty-five) left Mr. Taynton half a crown the poorer. Then the winner whirled his guest upstairs again to talk to his mother while he himself went round to

the stables to assure himself of the
well-being of the beloved motor.
Martin had already valeted it, after
its run, and was just locking up when
Morris arrived.

Morris gave his orders for next day
after a quite unnecessary examination
into the internal economy of the
beloved, and was just going back to
the house, when he paused, remembering something.

"Oh Martin," he said, "while I am
here, I want you to help in the house,
you know at dinner and so on, just
as you did to-night. And when there
are guests of mine here I want you
to look after them. For instance,
when Mr. Taynton goes to-night you
will be there to give him his hat and
coat. You 'll have rather a lot to do,
I 'm afraid."

Morris finished his cigarette and
went back to the drawing-room where
Mr. Taynton was already engaged in the

staid excitements of backgammon with his mother. That game over, Morris took his place, and before long the lawyer rose to go.

"Now I absolutely refuse to let you interrupt your game," he said. "I have found my way out of this house often enough, I should think. Good night, Mrs. Assheton. Good night Morris; don't break your neck my dear boy, in trying to break records."

Morris hardly attended to this, for the game was critical. He just rang the bell, said good night, and had thrown again before the door had closed behind Mr. Taynton. Below, in answer to the bell, was standing his servant.

Mr. Taynton looked at him again with some attention, and then glanced round to see if the discreet parlour-maids were about.

"So you are called Martin now," he observed gently.

"Yes, sir."

"I recognised you at once."

There was a short pause.

"Are you going to tell Mr. Morris, sir?" he asked.

"That I had to dismiss you two years ago for theft?" said Mr. Taynton quietly. "No, not if you behave yourself."

Mr. Taynton looked at him again kindly and sighed.

"No, let bygones be bygones," he said. "You will find your secret is safe enough. And, Martin, I hope you have really turned over a new leaf, and are living honestly now. That is so, my lad? Thank God; thank God. My umbrella? Thanks. Good night. No cab: I will walk."

## CHAPTER II

MR. TAYNTON lived in a square,
comfortable house in Montpellier Road, and thus, when he left
Mrs. Assheton's there was some two
miles of pavement and sea front between him and home. But the night
was of wonderful beauty, a night of
mid June, warm enough to make the
most cautious secure of chill, and at
the same time just made crisp with
a little breeze that blew or rather
whispered landward from over the
full-tide of the sleeping sea. High up in
the heavens swung a glorious moon,
which cast its path of white enchanted
light over the ripples, and seemed to
draw the heart even as it drew the
eyes heavenward. Mr. Taynton certainly, as he stepped out beneath the

stars, with the sea lying below him,
felt, in his delicate and sensitive
nature, the charm of the hour, and
being a good if not a brisk walker,
he determined to go home on foot.
And he stepped westward very con-
tentedly.

The evening, it would appear, had
much pleased him — for it was long
before his smile of retrospective pleasure faded from his pleasant mobile
face. Morris's trust and confidence in
him had been extraordinarily pleasant
to him: and modest and unassuming
as he was, he could not help a secret
gratification at the thought. What
a handsome fellow Morris was too, how
gay, how attractive! He had his
father's dark colouring, and tall figure,
but much of his mother's grace and
charm had gone to the modelling of
that thin sensitive mouth and the
long oval of his face. Yet there was
more of the father there, the father's

intense, almost violent, vitality was somehow more characteristic of the essential Morris than face or feature.

What a happy thing it was too — here the smile of pleasure illuminated Mr. Taynton's face again — that the boy whom he had dismissed two years before for some petty pilfering in his own house, should have turned out such a promising lad and should have found his way to so pleasant a berth as that of factotum to Morris. Kindly and charitable all through and ever eager to draw out the good in everybody and forgive the bad, Mr. Taynton had often occasion to deplore the hardness and uncharity of a world which remembers youthful errors and hangs them, like a mill-stone, round the neck of the offender, and it warmed his heart and kindled his smile to think of one case at any rate where a youthful misdemeanour was lived down and forgotten. At the time

he remembered being in doubt whether
he should not give the offender up
to justice, for the pilfering, petty
though it had been, had been somewhat persistent, but he had taken the
more merciful course, and merely dismissed the boy. He had been in
two minds about it before, wondering
whether it would not be better to
let Martin have a sharp lesson, but
to-night he was thankful that he had
not done so. The mercy he had
shown had come back to bless him
also; he felt a glow of thankfulness
that the subject of his clemency had
turned out so well. Punishment
often hardens the criminal, was one
of his settled convictions. But Morris — again his thoughts went back to
Morris, who was already standing on
the verge of manhood, on the verge,
too, he made no doubt of married life
and its joys and responsibilities. Mr.
Taynton was himself a bachelor, and

the thought gave him not a moment of jealousy, but a moment of void that ached a little at the thought of the common human bliss which he had himself missed. How charming, too, was the girl Madge Templeton, whom he had met, not for the first time, that evening. He himself had guessed how things stood between the two before Morris had confided in him, and it pleased him that his intuition was confirmed. What a pity, however, that the two were not going to meet next day, that she was out with her mother and would not get back till late. It would have been a cooling thought in the hot office hours of to-morrow to picture them sitting together in the garden at Falmer, or under one of the cool deep-foliaged oaks in the park.

Then suddenly his face changed, the smile faded, but came back next instant and broadened with a laugh.

And the man who laughs when he is by himself may certainly be supposed to have strong cause for amusement.

Mr. Taynton had come by this time to the West Pier, and a hundred yards farther would bring him to Montpellier Road. But it was yet early, as he saw (so bright was the moonlight) when he consulted his watch, and he retraced his steps some fifty yards, and eventually rang at the door of a big house of flats facing the sea, where his partner, who for the most part, looked after the London branch of their business, had his *pied-à-terre*. For the firm of Taynton and Mills was one of those respectable and solid businesses that, beginning in the country, had eventually been extended to town, and so far from its having its headquarters in town and its branch in Brighton, had its headquarters here and its branch in the metropolis. Mr. God-

frey Mills, so he learned at the door
had dined alone, and was in, and without further delay Mr. Taynton was
carried aloft in the gaudy bird-cage
of the lift, feeling sure that his partner would see him.

The flat into which he was ushered
with a smile of welcome from the man
who opened the door was furnished
with a sort of gross opulence that never
failed to jar on Mr. Taynton's exquisite
taste and cultivated mind. Pictures,
chairs, sofas, the patterns of the carpet,
and the heavy gilding of the cornices
were all sensuous, a sort of frangipanni
to the eye. The apparent contrast,
however, between these things and
their owner, was as great as that
between Mr. Taynton and his partner,
for Mr. Godfrey Mills was a thin, spare,
dark little man, brisk in movement,
with a look in his eye that betokened a
watchfulness and vigilance of the most
alert order. But useful as such a gift un-

doubtedly is, it was given to Mr. Godfrey
Mills perhaps a shade too obviously.
It would be unlikely that the stupidest
or shallowest person would give himself away when talking to him, for
it was so clear that he was always on
the watch for admission or information
that might be useful to him. He had,
however, the charm that a very active
and vivid mind always possesses, and
though small and slight, he was a figure
that would be noticed anywhere, so
keen and wide-awake was his face.
Beside him Mr. Taynton looked like a
benevolent country clergyman, more
distinguished for amiable qualities of
the heart, than intellectual qualities
of the head. Yet those — there were
not many of them — who in dealings
with the latter had tried to conduct
their business on these assumptions,
had invariably found it necessary to
reconsider their first impression of him.
His partner, however, was always con-

scious of a little impatience in talking to him; Taynton, he would have allowed, did not lack fine business qualities, but he was a little wanting in quickness.

Mills's welcome of him was abrupt.

"Pleased to see you," he said. "Cigar, drink? Sit down, won't you? What is it?"

"I dropped in for a chat on my way home," said Mr. Taynton. "I have been dining with Mrs. Assheton. A most pleasant evening. What a fine delicate face she has."

Mills bit off the end of a cigar.

"I take it that you did not come in merely to discuss the delicacy of Mrs. Assheton's face," he said.

"No, no, dear fellow; you are right to recall me. I too take it — I take it that you have found time to go over to Falmer yesterday. How did you find Sir Richard?"

"I found him well. I had a long talk with him."

"And you managed to convey something of those very painful facts which you felt it was your duty to bring to his notice?" asked Mr. Taynton.

Godfrey Mills laughed.

"I say, Taynton, is it really worth while keeping it up like this?" he asked. "It really saves so much trouble to talk straight, as I propose to do. I saw him, as I said, and I really managed remarkably well. I had these admissions wrung from me, I assure you it is no less than that, under promise of the most absolute secrecy. I told him young Assheton was leading an idle, extravagant, and dissipated life. I said I had seen him three nights ago in Piccadilly, not quite sober, in company with the class of person to whom one does not refer in polite society. Will that do?"

"Ah, I can easily imagine how painful you must have found ——" began Taynton.

But his partner interrupted.

"It was rather painful; you have spoken a true word in jest. I felt a brute, I tell you. But, as I pointed out to you, something of the sort was necessary."

Mr. Taynton suddenly dropped his slightly clerical manner.

"You have done excellently, my dear friend," he said. "And as you pointed out to me, it was indeed necessary to do something of the sort. I think by now, your revelations have already begun to take effect. Yes, I think I will take a little brandy and soda. Thank you very much."

He got up with greater briskness than he had hitherto shown.

"And you are none too soon," he said. "Morris, poor Morris, such a handsome fellow, confided to me this evening that he was in love with Miss Templeton. He is very much in earnest."

"And why do you think my interview has met with some success?" asked Mills.

"Well, it is only a conjecture, but when Morris asked if he might call any time to-morrow, Miss Templeton (who was also dining with Mrs. Assheton) said that she and her mother would be out all day and not get home till late. It does not strike me as being too fanciful to see in that some little trace perhaps of your handiwork."

"Yes, that looks like me," said Mills shortly.

Mr. Taynton took a meditative sip at his brandy and soda.

"My evening also has not been altogether wasted," he said. "I played what for me was a bold stroke, for as you know, my dear fellow, I prefer to leave to your nimble and penetrating mind things that want dash and boldness. But to-night, yes,

I was warmed with that wonderful port and was bold."

"What did you do?" asked Mills.

"Well, I asked, I almost implored dear Morris to give me two or three hours to-morrow and go through all the books, and satisfy himself everything is in order, and his investments well looked after. I told him also that the original £30,000 of his had, owing to judicious management, become £40,000. You see, that is unfortunately a thing past praying for. It is so indubitably clear from the earlier ledgers ——"

"But the port must indeed have warmed you," said Mills quickly. "Why, it was madness! What if he had consented?"

Mr. Taynton smiled.

"Ah, well, I in my slow synthetic manner had made up my mind that it was really quite impossible that he should consent to go into the books

and vouchers. To begin with, he has a
new motor car, and every hour spent
away from that car just now is to
his mind an hour wasted. Also, I
know him well. I knew that he
would never consent to spend several
hours over ledgers. Finally, even if
he had, though I knew from what I
know of him not that he would not but
that he *could* not, I could have — I
could have managed something. You
see, he knows nothing whatever about
business or investments."

Mills shook his head.

"But it was dangerous, anyhow,"
he said, "and I don't understand what
object could be served by it. It was
running a risk with no profit in view."

Then for the first time the inherent
strength of the quietness of the one
man as opposed to the obvious quickness and comprehension of the other
came into play.

"I think that I disagree with you

there, my dear fellow," said Mr. Taynton slowly, "though when I have
told you all, I shall be of course, as
always, delighted to recognise the
superiority of your judgment, should
you disagree with me, and convince
me of the correctness of your view.
It has happened, I know, a hundred
times before that you with your quick
intuitive perceptions have been right."

But his partner interrupted him.
He quite agreed with the sentiment,
but he wanted to learn without even
the delay caused by these compli-
mentary remarks, the upshot of
Taynton's rash proposal to Morris.

"What did young Assheton say?"
he asked.

"Well, my dear fellow," said
Taynton, "though I have really no
doubt that in principle I did a rash
thing, in actual practice my step
was justified, because Morris absolutely refused to look at the books.

Of course I know the young fellow well:
it argues no perspicuity on my part
to have foreseen that. And, I am
glad to say, something in my way of
putting it, some sincerity of manner
I suppose, gave rise to a fresh mark
of confidence in us on his part."

Mr. Taynton cleared his throat; his
quietness and complete absence of
hurry was so to speak, rapidly over-
hauling the quick, nimble mind of the
other.

"He asked me in fact to continue
being steward of his affairs in any
event. Should he marry to-morrow
I feel no doubt that he would not
spend a couple of minutes over his
financial affairs, unless, *unless*, as you
foresaw might happen, he had need
of a large lump sum. In that case,
my dear Mills, you and I would —
would find it impossible to live elsewhere than in the Argentine Republic,
were we so fortunate as to get there.

But, as far as this goes I only say that the step of mine which you felt to be dangerous has turned out most auspiciously. He begged me, in fact, to continue even after he came of age, acting for him at my present rate of remuneration."

Mr. Mills was listening to this with some attention. Here he laughed dryly.

"That is capital, then," he said. "You were right and I was wrong. God, Taynton, it's your manner you know, there's something of the country parson about you that is wonderfully convincing. You seem sincere without being sanctimonious. Why, if I was to ask young Assheton to look into his affairs for himself, he would instantly think there was something wrong, and that I was trying bluff. But when you do the same thing, that simple and perfectly correct explanation never occurs to him."

"No, dear Morris trusts me very completely," said Taynton, "But, then, if I may continue my little review of the situation, as it now stands, you and your talk with Sir Richard have vastly decreased the danger of his marrying. For, to be frank, I should not feel at all secure if that happened. Miss Templeton is an heiress herself, and Morris might easily take it into his head to spend ten or fifteen thousand pounds in building a house or buying an estate, and though I think I have guarded against his requiring an account of our stewardship, I can't prevent his wishing to draw a large sum of money. But your brilliant manœuvre may, we hope, effectually put a stop to the danger of his marrying Miss Templeton, and since I am convinced he is in love with her, why" — Mr. Taynton put his plump finger-tips together and raised his kind eyes to the ceil-

ing — "why, the chance of his wanting to marry anybody else is post-
poned anyhow, till, till he has got
over this unfortunate attachment.
In fact, my dear fellow, there is no
longer anything immediate to fear,
and I feel sure that before many
weeks are up, the misfortunes and ill
luck which for the last two years have
dogged us with such incredible per-
sistency will be repaired."

Mills said nothing for the moment
but splashed himself out a liberal
allowance of brandy into his glass, and
mixed it with a somewhat more carefully measured ration of soda. He
was essentially a sober man, but that
was partly due to the fact that his head
was as impervious to alcohol as teak is
to water, and it was his habit to indulge
in two, and those rather stiff, brandies
and sodas of an evening. He found
that they assisted and clarified thought.

"I wish to heaven you had n't

found it necessary to let young Assheton know that his £30,000 had increased to £40,000," he said. "That's £10,000 more to get back."

"Ah, it was just that which gave him, so he thought, such good cause for reposing complete confidence in me," remarked Mr. Taynton. "But as you say, it is £10,000 more to get back, and I should not have told him, were not certain ledgers of earlier years so extremely, extremely unmistakable on the subject."

"But if he is not going to look at ledgers at all ——" began Mills.

"Ah, the concealment of that sort of thing is one of the risks which it is not worth while to take," said the other, dropping for a moment the deferential attitude.

Mills was silent again. Then:

"Have you bought that option in Boston Coppers," he asked.

"Yes; I bought to-day."

Mills glanced at the clock as Mr. Taynton rose to go.

"Still only a quarter to twelve," he said. "If you have time, you might give me a detailed statement. I hardly know what you have done. It won't take a couple of minutes."

Mr. Taynton glanced at the clock likewise, and then put down his hat again.

"I can just spare the time," he said, "but I must get home by twelve; I have unfortunately come out without my latchkey, and I do not like keeping the servants up."

He pressed his fingers over his eyes a moment and then spoke.

Ten minutes later he was in the bird-cage of the lift again, and by twelve he had been admitted into his own house, apologising most amiably to his servant for having kept him up. There were a few letters for him and he opened and read those, then lit his bed-candle and went upstairs, but instead of undressing, sat for a full quarter of an hour in his arm-chair thinking. Then he spoke softly to himself.

"I think dear Mills means mischief in some way," he said. "But really for the moment it puzzles me to know what. However, I shall see to-morrow. Ah, I wonder if I guess!"

Then he went to bed, but contrary to custom did not get to sleep for a long time. But when he did there was a smile on his lips; a patient contented smile.

# CHAPTER III

MR. TAYNTON'S statement to his partner, which had taken him so few minutes to give, was of course concerned only with the latest financial operation which he had just embarked in, but for the sake of the reader it will be necessary to go a little further back, and give quite shortly the main features of the situation in which he and his partner found themselves placed.

Briefly then, just two years ago, at the time peace was declared in South Africa, the two partners of Taynton and Mills had sold out £30,000 of Morris Assheton's securities, which owing to their excellent management was then worth £40,000, and seeing a quite unrivalled opportunity of making

their fortunes, had become heavy pur-
chasers of South African mines, for
they reasoned that with peace once
declared it was absolutely certain that
prices would go up.  But, as is sometimes the way with absolute certain-
ties, the opposite had happened and
they had gone down.  They cut their
loss, however, and proceeded to buy
American rails.  In six months they
had entirely repaired the damage, and
seeing further unrivalled opportunities
from time to time, in buying motor-
car shares, in running a theatre and
other schemes, had managed a month
ago to lose all that was left of the
£30,000.  Being, therefore, already so
deeply committed, it was mere
prudence, the mere instinct of self-
preservation that had led them to sell
out the remaining £10,000, and to-day
Mr. Taynton had bought an option in
Boston copper with it.  The manner
of an option is as follows:

Boston Copper to-day was quoted at £5 10s 6d, and by paying a premium of twelve shillings and sixpence per share, they were entitled to buy Boston Copper shares any time within the next three months at a price of £6 3s. Supposing therefore (as Mr. Taynton on very good authority had supposed) that Boston Copper, a rapidly improving company, rose a couple of points within the next three months, and so stood at £7 10s 6d; he had the right of exercising his option and buying them at £6 3s thus making £1 7s 6d per share. But a higher rise than this was confidently expected, and Taynton, though not really of an over sanguine disposition, certainly hoped to make good the greater part if not all of their somewhat large defalcations. He had bought an option of 20,000 shares, the option of which cost (or would cost at the end of those months) rather over £10,000.

In other words, the moment that the shares rose to a price higher than £6 3s, all further appreciation was pure gain. If they did not rise so high, he would of course not exercise the option, and sacrifice the money.

That was certainly a very unpleasant thing to contemplate, but it had been more unpleasant when, so far as he knew, Morris was on the verge of matrimony, and would then step into the management of his own affairs. But bad though it all was, the situation had certainly been immensely ameliorated this evening, since on the one hand his partner had, it was not unreasonable to hope, said to Madge's father things about Morris that made his marriage with Madge exceedingly unlikely, while on the other hand, even if it happened, his affairs, according to his own wish, would remain in Mr. Taynton's hands with the same completeness as here-

tofore. It would, of course, be necessary to pay him his income, and
though this would be a great strain
on the finances of the two partners,
it was manageable. Besides (Mr.
Taynton sincerely hoped that this
would not be necessary) the money
which was Mrs. Assheton's for her
lifetime was in his hands also, so if
the worst came to the worst ——

Now the composition and nature
of the extraordinary animal called
man is so unexpected and unlikely
that any analysis of Mr. Taynton's
character may seem almost grotesque.
It is a fact nevertheless that his was a
nature capable of great things, it is
also a fact that he had long ago been
deeply and bitterly contrite for the
original dishonesty of using the money
of his client. But by aid of those
strange perversities of nature, he had
by this time honestly and sincerely

got to regard all their subsequent
employments of it merely as efforts
on his part to make right an original
wrong. He wanted to repair his fault,
and it seemed to him that to commit
it again was the only means at his
disposal for doing so. A strain, too,
of Puritan piety was bound up in the
constitution of his soul, and in private
life he exercised high morality, and
was also kind and charitable. He
belonged to guilds and societies that
had as their object the improvement
and moral advancement of young
men. He was a liberal patron of
educational schemes, he sang a fer-
vent and fruity tenor in the choir of
St. Agnes, he was a regular communicant,
his nature looked toward good, and
turned its eyes away from evil. To do
him justice he was not a hypocrite,
though, if all about him were known,
and a plebiscite taken, it is probable
that he would be unanimously con-

demned.  Yet the universal opinion
would be wrong:  he was no hypocrite,
but only had the bump of self-preservation enormously developed.  He had
cheated and swindled, but he was
genuinely opposed to cheating and
swindling.  He was cheating and
swindling now, in buying the option
of Boston Copper.  But he did not
know that:  he wanted to repair the
original wrong, to hand back to Morris
his fortune unimpaired, and also to
save himself.  But of these two wants,
the second, it must be confessed, was
infinitely the stronger.  To save himself there was perhaps nothing that
he would stick at.  However, it was
his constant wish and prayer that he
might not be led into temptation.
He knew well what his particular
temptation was, namely this instinct
of self-preservation, and constantly
thought and meditated about it.  He
knew that he was hardly himself

when the stress of it came on him;
it was like a possession.

Mills, though an excellent partner
and a man of most industrious habits,
had, so Mr. Taynton would have admitted, one little weak spot. He
never was at the office till rather late
in the morning. True, when he came,
he soon made up for lost time, for he
was possessed, as we have seen, of
a notable quickness and agility of
mind, but sometimes Taynton found
that he was himself forced to be
idle till Mills turned up, if his signature or what not was required for
papers before work could be further
proceeded with. This, in fact, was
the case next morning, and from half
past eleven Mr. Taynton had to sit
idly in his office, as far as the work
of the firm was concerned until his
partner arrived. It was a little tire-
some that this should happen to-day,

because there was nothing else that
need detain him, except those deeds
for the execution of which his partner's
signature was necessary, and he could,
if only Mills had been punctual, have
gone out to Rottingdean before lunch,
and inspected the Church school there
in the erection of which he had taken
so energetic an interest. Timmins,
however, the gray-haired old head
clerk, was in the office with him, and
Mr. Taynton always liked a chat with
Timmins.

"And the grandson just come home,
has he Mr. Timmins?" he was saying.
"I must come and see him. Why
he'll be six years old, won't he, by
now?"

"Yes, sir, turned six."

"Dear me, how time goes on! The
morning is going on, too, and still Mr.
Mills isn't here."

He took a quill pen and drew a
half sheet of paper toward him, poised

his pen a moment and then wrote quickly.

"What a pity I can't sign for him," he said, passing his paper over to the clerk. "Look at that; now even you, Timmins, though you have seen Mr. Mills's handwriting ten thousand times, would be ready to swear that the signature was his, would you not?"

Timmins looked scrutinisingly at it.

"Well, I'm sure, sir! What a forger you would have made!" he said admiringly. "I would have sworn that was Mr. Mills's own hand of write. It's wonderful, sir."

Mr. Taynton sighed, and took the paper again.

"Yes, it is like, isn't it?" he said, "and it's so easy to do. Luckily forgers don't know the way to forge properly."

"And what might that be, sir?" asked Timmins.

"Why, to throw yourself mentally into the nature of the man whose handwriting you wish to forge. Of course one has to know the handwriting thoroughly well, but if one does that one just has to visualise it, and then, as I said, project oneself into the other, not laboriously copy the handwriting. Let's try another. Ah, who is that letter from? Mrs. Assheton is n't it. Let me look at the signature just once again."

Mr. Taynton closed his eyes a moment after looking at it. Then he took his quill, and wrote quickly.

"You would swear to that, too, would you not, Timmins?" he asked.

"Why, God bless me yes, sir," said he. "Swear to it on the book."

The door opened and as Godfrey Mills came in, Mr. Taynton tweaked the paper out of Timmins's hand, and tore it up. It might perhaps seem strange to dear Mills that his partner had been forging his signature, though only in jest.

"'Fraid I 'm rather late," said Mills.

"Not at all, my dear fellow," said Taynton without the slightest touch of ill-humour. "How are you? There's very little to do; I want your signature to this and this, and your careful perusal of that. Mrs. Assheton's letter? No, that only concerns me; I have dealt with it."

A quarter of an hour was sufficient, and at the end Timmins carried the papers away leaving the two partners together. Then, as soon as the door closed, Mills spoke.

"I 've been thinking over our conversation of last night," he said, "and there are some points I don't think you have quite appreciated, which I should like to put before you."

Something inside Mr. Taynton's brain, the same watcher perhaps who looked at Morris so closely the evening before, said to him. "He is going to try it on." But it was not the watcher but his normal self that answered. He beamed gently on his partner.

"My dear fellow, I might have been sure that your quick mind would have seen new aspects, new combinations," he said.

Mills leaned forward over the table.

"Yes, I have seen new aspects, to adopt your words," he said, "and I will put them before you. These financial operations, shall we call them, have been going on for two years now, have they not? You began by losing a large sum in South Africans ——"

"We began," corrected Mr. Taynton, gently. He was looking at the other quite calmly; his face expressed no surprise at all; if there was anything in his expression beyond that of quiet kindness, it was perhaps pity.

"I said 'you,'" said Mills in a hectoring tone, "and I will soon explain why. You lost a large sum in South Africans, but won it back again in Americans.

You then again, and again contrary
to my advice, embarked in perfect
wild-cat affairs, which ended in our —
I say 'our' here — getting severely
scratched and mauled. Altogether
you have frittered away £30,000, and
have placed the remaining ten in a
venture which to my mind is as wild
as all the rest of your unfortunate
ventures. These speculations have,
almost without exception, been choices
of your own, not mine. That was
*one* of the reasons why I said 'you,'
not 'we.'"

He paused a moment.

"Another reason is," he said, "because without any exception the transactions have taken place on your advice
and in your name, not in mine."

That was a sufficiently meaning
statement, but Mills did not wish his
partner to be under any misappre-
hension as to what he implied.

"In other words," he said, "I can

deny absolutely all knowledge of the whole of those operations."

Mr. Taynton gave a sudden start, as if the significance of this had only this moment dawned on him, as if he had not understood the first statement. Then he seemed to collect himself.

"You can hardly do that," he said, "as I hold letters of yours which imply such knowledge."

Mills smiled rather evilly.

"Ah, it is not worth while bluffing," he said. "I have never written such a letter to you. You know it. Is it likely I should?"

Mr. Taynton apparently had no reply to this. But he had a question to ask.

"Why are you taking up this hostile and threatening attitude?"

"I have not meant to be hostile, and I have certainly not threatened," replied Mills. "I have put before you, quite dispassionately I hope, certain facts. Indeed I should say it was you who had threatened in the matter of those letters, which, unhappily, have never existed at all. I will proceed."

"Now what has been my part in this affair? I have observed you lost money in speculations of which I disapproved, but you always knew best. I have advanced money to you before now to tide over embarrassments that would otherwise have been disastrous. By the exercise of diplomacy — or lying — yesterday, I averted a very grave danger. I point out to you also that there is nothing to implicate me in these — these fraudulent employments of a client's money. So I ask, where I come in? What do I get by it?"

Mr. Taynton's hands were trembling as he fumbled at some papers on his desk.

"You know quite well that we are to share all profits?" he said.

"Yes, but at present there have not been any. I have been, to put it plainly, pulling you out of holes. And I think — I think my trouble ought to be remunerated. I sincerely hope you will take that view also. Or shall I remind you again that there is nothing in the world to connect me with these, well, frauds?"

Mr. Taynton got up from his chair, strolled across to the window where he drew down the blind a little, so as to shut out the splash of sunlight that fell on his table.

"You have been betting again, I suppose," he asked quietly.

"Yes, and have been unfortunate. Pray do not trouble to tell me again how foolish it is to gamble like that. You may be right. I have no doubt you are right. But I think one has as much right to gamble with one's own money as to do so with the money of other people."

This apparently seemed unanswerable; anyhow Mr. Taynton made no reply. Then, having excluded the splash of sunlight he sat down again.

"You have not threatened, you tell me," he said, "but you have pointed out to me that there is no evidence that you have had a hand in certain transactions. You say that I know you have helped me in these transactions; you say you require remuneration for your services. Does not that, I ask, imply a threat? Does it not mean that you are blackmailing me? Else why should you bring these facts — I do not dispute them — to my notice? Supposing I refuse you remuneration?"

Mills had noted the signs of agitation and anxiety. He felt that he was on safe ground. The black-mailer lives entirely on the want of courage in his victims.

"You will not, I hope, refuse me remuneration," he said. "I have not threatened you yet, because I feel sure you will be wise. I might, of course, subsequently threaten you."

Again there was silence. Mr. Taynton had picked up a quill pen, the same with which he had been writing before, for the nib was not yet dry.

"The law is rather severe on black-mailers," he remarked.

"It is. Are you going to bring an action against me for blackmail? Will not that imply the re-opening of — of certain ledgers, which we agreed last night had better remain shut?"

Again there was silence. There was a completeness in this reasoning which rendered comment superfluous.

"How much do you want?" asked Mr. Taynton.

Mills was not so foolish as to "breathe a sigh of relief." But he noted with satisfaction that there was no sign of fight in his adversary and partner.

"I want two thousand pounds," he said, "at once."

"That is a large sum."

"It is. If it were a small sum I should not trouble you."

Mr. Taynton again got up and strayed aimlessly about the room.

"I can't give it you to-day," he said. "I shall have to sell out some stock."

"I am not unreasonable about a reasonable delay," said Mills.

"You are going to town this afternoon?"

"Yes, I must. There is a good deal of work to be done. It will take me all to-morrow."

"And you will be back the day after to-morrow?"

"Yes, I shall be back here that night, that is to say, I shall not get away from town till the afternoon. I should like your definite answer then, if it is not inconvenient. I could come and see you that night, the day after to-morrow — if you wished."

Mr. Taynton thought over this with his habitual deliberation.

"You will readily understand that all friendly relations between us are quite over," he said. "You have done a cruel and wicked thing, but I don't see how I can resist it. I should like, however, to have a little further talk about it, for which I have not time now."

Mills rose.

"By all means," he said. "I do not suppose I shall be back here till nine in the evening. I have had no exercise lately, and I think very

likely I shall get out of the train at
Falmer, and walk over the downs."

Mr. Taynton's habitual courtesy came
to his aid. He would have been
polite to a thief or a murderer, if he
met him socially.

"Those cool airs of the downs are
very invigorating." he said. "I will
not expect you therefore till half past
nine that night. I shall dine at home,
and be alone."

"Thanks. I must be going. I shall
only just catch my train to town."

Mills nodded a curt gesture of fare-
well, and left the room, and when he
had gone Mr. Taynton sat down again
in the chair by the table, and remained
there some half hour. He knew well
the soundness of his partner's reasoning; all he had said was fatally and
abominably true. There was no way
out of it. Yet to pay money to a
blackmailer was, to the legal mind,
a confession of guilt. Innocent people,

unless they were abject fools, did not pay blackmail. They prosecuted the blackmailer. Yet here, too, Mills's simple reasoning held good. He could not prosecute the blackmailer, since he was not in the fortunate position of being innocent. But if you paid a blackmailer once, you were for ever in his power. Having once yielded, it was necessary to yield again. He must get some assurance that no further levy would take place. He must satisfy himself that he would be quit of all future danger from this quarter. Yet from whence was such assurance to come? He might have it a hundred times over in Godfrey Mills's handwriting, but he could never produce that as evidence, since again the charge of fraudulent employment of clients' money would be in the air. No doubt, of course, the blackmailer would be sentenced, but the cause of blackmail would necessarily be public.   No, there was no way out.

Two thousand pounds, though! Frugally and simply as he lived, that was to him a dreadful sum, and represented the savings of at least eighteen months.   This meant that there was for him another eighteen months of work, just when he hoped to see his retirement coming close to him.   Mills demanded that he should work an extra year and a half, and out of those few years that in all human probability still remained to him in this pleasant world.   Yet there was no way out!

Half an hour's meditation convinced him of this, and, as was his sensible plan, when a thing was inevitable, he never either fought against it nor wasted energy in regretting it.   And he went slowly out of the office into which he had come so briskly an hour or two before.   But his face expressed no sign of disquieting emotion; he nodded kindly to Timmins, and endorsed his desire to be allowed to come and see the grandson. If anything was on his mind, or if he was revolving some policy for the future, it did not seem to touch or sour that kindly, pleasant face.

## CHAPTER IV

MR. TAYNTON did not let these very unpleasant occurrences interfere with the usual and beneficent course of his life, but faced the crisis with that true bravery that not only meets a thing without flinching, but meets it with the higher courage of cheerfulness, serenity and ordinary behaviour. He spent the rest of the day in fact in his usual manner, enjoying his bathe before lunch, his hour of the paper and the quiet cigar afterward, his stroll over the springy turf of the downs, and he enjoyed also the couple of hours of work that brought him to dinner time. Then afterward he spent his evening, as was his weekly custom, at the club for young men which he had founded, where instead of being exposed to the evening lures of the sea-front and the public house, they could spend (on payment of a really nominal subscription) a quieter and more innocent hour over chess, bagatelle and the illustrated papers, or if more energetically disposed, in the airy gymnasium adjoining the reading-room, where they could indulge in friendly rivalry with boxing gloves or single-stick, or feed the appetites of their growing muscles with dumb-bells and elastic contrivances. Mr. Taynton had spent a couple of hours there, losing a game of chess to one youthful adversary, but getting back his laurels over bagatelle, and before he left, had arranged for a geological expedition to visit, on the Whitsuntide bank holiday next week, the curious raised beach which protruded so remarkably from the range of chalk downs some ten miles away.

On returning home, it is true he had
6

deviated a little from his usual habits, for instead of devoting the half-hour before bed-time to the leisurely perusal of the evening paper, he had merely given it one glance, observing that copper was strong and that Boston Copper in particular had risen half a point, and had then sat till bed-time doing nothing whatever, a habit to which he was not generally addicted.

He was seated in his office next morning and was in fact on the point of leaving for his bathe, for this hot genial June was marching on its sunny way uninterrupted by winds or rain, when Mr. Timmins, after discreetly tapping, entered, and closed the door behind him.

"Mr. Morris Assheton, sir, to see you," he said. "I said I would find out if you were disengaged, and could hardly restrain him from coming in with me. The young gentleman seems very excited and agitated. Hardly himself, sir."

"Indeed, show him in," said Mr. Taynton.

A moment afterward the door burst open and banged to again behind Morris. High colour flamed in his face, his black eyes sparkled with vivid dangerous light, and he had no salutation for his old friend.

"I 've come on a very unpleasant business," he said, his voice not in control.

Mr. Taynton got up. He had only had one moment of preparation and he thought, at any rate, that he knew for certain what this unpleasant business must be. Evidently Mills had given him away. For what reason he had done so he could not guess; after his experience of yesterday it might have been from pure devilry, or again he might have feared that in desperation, Taynton would take that extreme step of prosecuting him for blackmail. But, for that moment

Taynton believed that Morris's agitation must be caused by this, and it says much for the iron of his nerve that he did not betray himself by a tremor.

"My dear Morris," he said, "I must ask you to pull yourself together. You are out of your own control. Sit down, please, and be silent for a minute. Then tell me calmly what is the matter.

Morris sat down as he was told, but the calmness was not conspicuous.

"Calm?" he said. "Would you be calm in my circumstances, do you think?"

"You have not yet told me what they are," said Mr. Taynton.

"I 've just seen Madge Templeton," he said. "I met her privately by appointment. And she told me — she told me ——"

Master of himself though he was, Mr. Taynton had one moment of physical giddiness, so complete and sudden

was the revulsion and reaction that
took place in his brain. A moment
before he had known, he thought, for
certain that his own utter ruin was
imminent. Now he knew that it was
not that, and though he had made
one wrong conjecture as to what the
unpleasant business was, he did not
think that his second guess was far
astray.

"Take your time, Morris," he said.
"And, my dear boy, try to calm yourself. You say I should not be calm in
your circumstances. Perhaps I should
not, but I should make an effort.
Tell me everything slowly, omitting
nothing."

This speech, combined with the
authoritative personality of Mr.
Taynton, had an extraordinary effect
on Morris. He sat quiet a moment or
two, then spoke.

"Yes, you are quite right," he said,
"and after all I have only conjecture

to go on yet, and I have been behaving as if it was proved truth. God! if it is proved to be true, though, I 'll expose him, I 'll — I 'll horsewhip him, I 'll murder him!"

Mr. Taynton slapped the table with his open hand.

"Now, Morris, none of these wild words," he said. "I will not listen to you for a moment, if you do not control yourself."

Once again, and this time more permanently the man's authority asserted itself. Morris again sat silent for a time, then spoke evenly and quietly.

"Two nights ago you were dining with us," he said, "and Madge was there. Do you remember my asking her if I might come to see them, and she said she and her mother would be out all day?"

"Yes; I remember perfectly," said Mr. Taynton.

"Well, yesterday afternoon I was motoring by the park, and I saw Madge sitting on the lawn. I stopped the motor and watched. She sat there for nearly an hour, and then Sir Richard came out of the house and they walked up and down the lawn together."

"Ah, you must have been mistaken," said Mr. Taynton. "I know the spot you mean on the road, where you can see the lawn, but it's half a mile off. It must have been some friend of hers perhaps staying in the house."

Morris shook his head.

"I was not mistaken," he said. "For yesterday evening I got a note from her, saying she had posted it secretly, but that she must see me, though she was forbidden to do so, or to hold any communication with me."

"Forbidden?" ejaculated Mr. Taynton.

"Yes, forbidden.  Well, this morning I went to the place she named, outside on the downs beyond the park gate and saw her.  Somebody has been telling vile lies about me to her father.  I think I know who it is."

Mr. Taynton held up his hand.

"Stop," he said, "let us have your conjecture afterward.  Tell me first not what you guess, but what happened.  Arrange it all in your mind, tell it me as connectedly as you can."

Morris paused a moment.

"Well, I met Madge as I told you, and this was her story.  Three days ago she and her father and mother were at lunch, and they had been talking in the most friendly way about me, and it was arranged to ask me to spend all yesterday with them. Madge, as you know, the next night was dining with us, and it was agreed that she should ask me verbally.

After lunch she and her father went out riding, and when they returned they found that your partner Mills, had come to call. He stayed for tea, and after tea had a talk alone with Sir Richard, while she and her mother sat out on the lawn. Soon after he had gone, Sir Richard sent for Lady Templeton, and it was nearly dressing-time when she left him again. She noticed at dinner that both her father and mother seemed very grave, and when Madge went up to bed, her mother said that perhaps they had better not ask me over, as there was some thought of their being away all day. Also if I suggested coming over, when Madge dined with us, she was to give that excuse. That was all she was told for the time being."

Morris paused again.

"You are telling this very clearly and well, my dear boy," said the lawyer, very gravely and kindly.

"It is so simple," said he with a
biting emphasis. "Then next morning after breakfast her father sent for
her. He told her that they had
learned certain things about me which
made them think it better not to see
any more of me. What they were,
she was not told, but, I was not, it
appeared, the sort of person with
whom they chose to associate. Now,
before God, those things that they
were told, whatever they were, were
lies. I lead a straight and sober life."

Mr. Taynton was attending very
closely.

"Thank God, Madge did not believe
a word of it," said Morris, his face
suddenly flushing, "and like a brick,
and a true friend she wrote at once
to me, as I said, in order to tell me
all this. We talked over, too, who it
could have been who had said these
vile things to her father. There was
only one person who could. She had

ridden with her father till tea-time. Then came your partner. Sir Richard saw nobody else; nobody else called that afternoon; no post came in."

Mr. Taynton had sprung up and was walking up and down the room in great agitation.

"I can't believe that," he said. "There must be some other explanation. Godfrey Mills say those things about you! It is incredible. My dear boy, until it is proved, you really must not let yourself believe that to be possible. You can't believe such wickedness against a man, one, too, whom I have known and trusted for years, on no evidence. There is no direct evidence yet. Let us leave that alone for the moment. What are you going to do now?"

"I came here to see him," said Morris. "But I am told he is away. So I thought it better to tell you."

"Yes, quite right. And what else?"

"I have written to Sir Richard, demanding, in common justice, that he should see me, should tell me what he has heard against me, and who told him. I don't think he will refuse. I don't see how he can refuse. I have asked him to see me to-morrow afternoon."

Mr. Taynton mentally examined this in all its bearings. Apparently it satisfied him.

"You have acted wisely and providently," he said. "But I want to beg you, until you have definite information, to forbear from thinking that my dear Mills could conceivably have been the originator of these scandalous tales, tales which I know from my knowledge of you are impossible to be true. From what I know of him, however, it is impossible he could have said such things. I cannot believe him capable of a mean or deceitful action, and that he should be guilty of such unfathomable ini-

quity is simply out of the question.
You must assume him innocent till
his guilt is proved."

"But who else could it have been?'
cried Morris, his voice rising again.

"It could not have been he," said
Taynton firmly.

There was a long silence; then
Morris rose.

"There is one thing more," he said,
"which is the most important of all.
This foul scandal about me, of course,
I know will be cleared up, and I shall
be competent to deal with the offender.
But — but Madge and I said other
things to each other. I told her what
I told you, that I loved her. And
she loves me."

The sternness, the trouble, the anxiety
all melted from Mr. Taynton's face.

"Ah, my dear fellow, my dear
fellow," he said with outstretched
hands. Thank you for telling me. I
am delighted, overjoyed, and indeed,

as you say, that is far more important than anything else. My dear Morris, and is not your mother charmed?"

Morris shook his head.

"I have not told her yet, and I shall not till this is cleared up. It is her birthday the day after to-morrow; perhaps I shall be able to tell her then."

He rose.

"I must go," he said. "And I will do all I can to keep my mind off accusing him, until I know. But when I think of it, I see red."

Mr. Taynton patted his shoulder affectionately.

"I should have thought that you had got something to think about, which would make it easy for you to prevent your thoughts straying elsewhere," he said.

"I shall need all the distractions I can get," said Morris rather grimly.

Morris walked quickly back along

the sea front toward Sussex Square,
and remembered as he went that he had
not yet bought any gift for his mother
on her birthday. There was something, too, which she had casually
said a day or two ago that she wanted,
what was it? Ah, yes, a new blotting-
book for her writing-table in the
drawing-room. The shop she habitu-
ally dealt at for such things, a branch
of Asprey's, was only a few yards
farther on, and he turned in to make
inquiries as to whether she had
ordered it. It appeared that she had
been in that very morning, but the
parcel had not been sent yet. So
Morris, taking the responsibility on
himself, counterordered the plain red
morocco book she had chosen, and
chose another, with fine silver scroll-
work at the corners. He ordered, too,
that a silver lettered inscription should
be put on it. "H. A. from M. A." with
the date, two days ahead, "June 24th,

1905." This he gave instructions should
be sent to the house on the morning
of June 24th, the day after to-morrow.
He wished it to be sent so as to arrive
with the early post on that morning.

The promise which Morris had made
his old friend not to let his thoughts
dwell on suspicion and conjecture as
yet uncertain of foundation was one
of those promises which are made in
absolute good faith, but which in
their very nature cannot be kept.
The thought of the hideous treachery,
the gratuitous falsehood, of which, in
his mind, he felt convinced Godfrey
Mills had been guilty was like blood
soaking through a bandage. All that
he could do was to continue putting
on fresh bandages—that was all
of his promise that he was able to
fulfill, and in spite of the bandages the
blood stained and soaked its way
through. In the afternoon he took

out the motor, but his joy in it for the time was dead, and it was only because in the sense of pace and swift movement he hoped to find a narcotic to thought, that he went out at all. But there was no narcotic there, nor even in the thought of this huge joy of love that had dawned on him was there forgetfulness for all else, joy and sorrow and love, were for the present separated from him by these hideous and libellous things that had been said about him. Until they were removed, until they passed into non-existence again, nothing had any significance for him. Everything was coloured with them; bitterness as of blood tinged everything. Hours, too, must pass before they could be removed; this long midsummer day had to draw to its end, night had to pass; the hour of early dawn, the long morning had to be numbered with the past before he could even learn who was responsible for this poisoned tale.

And when he learned, or rather when his conjecture was confirmed as to who it was (for his supposition was conjecture in the sense that it only wanted the actual seal of reality on it) what should he do next? Or rather what must he do next? He felt that when he knew absolutely for certain who had said this about him, a force of indignation and hatred, which at present he kept chained up, must infallibly break its chain, and become merely a wild beast let loose. He felt he would be no longer responsible for what he did, something had to happen; something more than mere apology or retraction of words. To lie and slander like that was a crime, an insult against human and divine justice. It would be nothing for the criminal to say he was sorry; he had to be punished. A man who did that was not fit to live; he was a man no longer, he was a biting, poisonous reptile, who for the sake of the community must be expunged. Yet human justice which hanged people for violent crimes committed under great provocation, dealt more lightly with this far more devilish thing, a crime committed coldly and calculatingly, that had planned not the mere death of his body, but the disgrace and death of his character. Godfrey Mills—he checked the word and added to himself "if it was he"—had morally tried to kill him.

Morris, after his interview that morning with Mr. Taynton, had lunched alone in Sussex Square, his mother having gone that day up to London for two nights. His plan had been to go up with her, but he had excused himself on the plea of business with his trustees, and she had gone alone. Directly after lunch he had taken the motor out, and had whirled along the coast road, past Rottingdean through Newhaven and Seaford, and ten miles farther until the suburbs of East-bourne had begun. There he turned, his thoughts still running a mill-race in his head, and retracing his road had by now come back to within a mile of Brighton again. The sun gilded the smooth channel, the winds were still, the hot midsummer afternoon lay heavy on the land. Then he stopped the motor and got out, telling Martin to wait there.

He walked over the strip of velvety down grass to the edge of the white cliffs, and there sat down. The sea below him whispered and crawled, above the sun was the sole tenant of the sky, and east and west the down was empty of passengers. He, like his soul, was alone, and alone he had to think these things out.

Yes, this liar and slanderer, whoever

he was, had tried to kill him. The attempt had been well-planned too, for the chances had been a thousand to one in favour of the murderer. But the one chance had turned up, Madge had loved him, and she had been brave, setting at defiance the order of her father, and had seen him secretly, and told him all the circumstances of this attack on him. But supposing she had been just a shade less brave, supposing her filial obedience had weighed an ounce heavier? Then he would never have known anything about it. The result would simply have been, as it was meant to be, that the Templetons were out when he called. There would have been a change of subject in their rooms when his name was mentioned, other people would have vaguely gathered that Mr. Morris Assheton's name was not productive of animated conversation; their gatherings would have spread further, while he himself, ignorant of all cause, would have encountered cold shoulders.

Morris's hands clutched at the short down grass, tearing it up and scattering it. He was helpless, too, unless he took the law into his own hands. It would do no good, young as he was, he knew that, to bring any action for defamation of character, since the world only says, if a man justifies himself by the only legal means in his power, "There must have been something in it, since it was said!" No legal remedy, no fines or, even imprisonment, far less apology and retraction satisfied justice. There were only two courses open: one to regard the slander as a splash of mud thrown by some vile thing that sat in the gutter, and simply ignore it; the other to do something himself, to strike, to hit, with his bodily hands, whatever the result of his violence was.

He felt his shoulder-muscles rise and brace themselves at the thought, all the strength and violence of his young manhood, with its firm sinews and supple joints, told him that it was his willing and active servant and would do his pleasure. He wanted to smash the jaw bone that had formed these lies, and he wanted the world to know he had done so. Yet that was not enough, he wanted to throttle the throat from which the words had come; the man ought to be killed; it was right to kill him just as it was right to kill a poisonous snake that somehow disguised itself as a man, and was received into the houses of men.

Indeed, should Morris be told, as he felt sure he would be, who his slanderer and defamer was, that gentleman would be wise to keep out of his way with him in such a mood. There was danger and death abroad on this calm hot summer afternoon.

# CHAPTER V

IT WAS about four o'clock on the afternoon of the following day, and Mr. Taynton was prolonging his hour of quietude after lunch, and encroaching thereby into the time he daily dedicated to exercise. It was but seldom that he broke into the routine of habits so long formed, and indeed the most violent rain or snow of winter, the most cutting easterly blasts of March, never, unless he had some definite bodily ailment, kept him indoors or deprived him of his brisk health-giving trudge over the downs or along the sea front. But occasionally when the weather was unusually hot, he granted himself the indulgence of sitting still instead of walking, and certainly to-day the least lenient judge might say that there were strong extenuating circumstances in his favour. For the heat of the past week had been piling itself up, like the heaped waters of flood and this afternoon was intense in its heat, its stillness and sultriness. It had been sunless all day, and all day the blanket of clouds that beset the sky had been gathering themselves into blacker and more ill-omened density. There would certainly be a thunderstorm before morning, and the approach of it made Mr. Taynton feel that he really had not the energy to walk. By and by perhaps he might be tempted to go in quest of coolness along the sea front, or perhaps later in the evening he might, as he sometimes did, take a carriage up on to the downs, and come gently home to a late supper. He would have time for that to-day, for according to arrangement his partner was to drop in about half past nine that evening. If he got back at nine, supposing he went at all, he would have time to have some food before receiving him.

He sat in a pleasant parquetted room looking out into the small square garden at the back of his house in Montpellier Road. Big awnings stretched from the window over the broad gravel path outside, and in spite of the excessive heat the room was full of dim coolness. There was but little furniture in it, and it presented the strongest possible contrast to the appointments of his partner's flat with its heavy decorations, its somewhat gross luxury. A few water-colours hung on the white walls, a few Persian rugs strewed the floor, a big bookcase with china on the top filled one end of the room, his writing-table, a half dozen of Chippendale chairs, and the chintz-covered sofa where he now lay practically completed the inventory of the room. Three or four bronzes, a Narcissus, a fifteenth-century Italian

St. Francis, and a couple of Greek reproductions stood on the chimney-piece, but the whole room breathed an atmosphere of æsthetic asceticism.

Since lunch Mr. Taynton had glanced at the paper, and also looked up the trains from Lewes in order to assure himself that he need not expect his partner till half past nine, and since then, though his hands and his eyes had been idle, his mind had been very busy.  Yet for all its business, he had not arrived at much.  Morris, Godfrey Mills, and himself; he had placed these three figures in all sorts of positions in his mind, and yet every combination of them was somehow terrible and menacing.  Try as he would he could not construct a peaceful or secure arrangement of them.  In whatever way he grouped them there was danger.

The kitchen passage ran out at right angles to the room in which he sat, and formed one side of the garden. The windows in it were high up, so that it did not overlook the flower-beds, and on this torrid afternoon they were all fully open. Suddenly from just inside came the fierce clanging peal of a bell, which made him start from his recumbent position. It was the front-door bell, as he knew, and as it continued ringing as if a maniac's grip was on the handle, he heard the steps of his servant running along the stone floor of the passage to see what imperative summons this was. Then, as the front door was opened, the bell ceased as suddenly as it had begun, and the moment afterward he heard Morris's voice shrill and commanding.

"But he has got to see me," he cried, "What's the use of you going to ask if he will?"

Mr. Taynton went to the door of his room which opened into the hall.

"Come in, Morris," he said.

Though it had been Morris's hand which had raised so uncontrolled a clamour, and his voice that just now had been so uncontrolled, there was no sign, when the door of Mr. Taynton's room had closed behind them, that there was any excitement of any sort raging within him. He sat down at once in a chair opposite the window, and Mr. Taynton saw that in spite of the heat of the day and the violence of that storm which he knew was yelling and screaming through his brain, his face was absolutely white. He sat with his hands on the arms of the Chippendale chair, and they too were quite still.

"I have seen Sir Richard," said he, "and I came back at once to see you. He has told me everything. Godfrey Mills has been lying about me and slandering me."

Mr. Taynton sat down heavily on the sofa.

"No, no; don't say it, don't say it," he murmured. "It can't be true, I can't believe it."

"But it is true, and you have got to believe it. He suggested that you should go and talk it over with him. I will drive you up in the car, if you wish ——"

Mr. Taynton waved his hand with a negative gesture.

"No, no, not at once," he cried. "I must think it over. I must get used to this dreadful, this appalling shock. I am utterly distraught."

Morris turned to him, and across his face for one moment there shot, swift as a lightning-flash, a quiver of rage so rabid that he looked scarcely human, but like some Greek present-ment of the Furies or Revenge. Never, so thought his old friend, had he seen such glorious youthful beauty so instinct and inspired with hate. It was the demoniacal force of that which lent such splendour to it. But it passed in a second, and Morris still very pale, very quiet spoke to him.

"Where is he?" he asked. "I must see him at once. It won't keep."

Then he sprang up, his rage again mastering him.

"What shall I do it with?" he said. "What shall I do it with?"

For the moment Mr. Taynton forgot himself and his anxieties.

"Morris, you don't know what you are saying," he cried. "Thank God nobody but me heard you say that!"

Morris seemed not to be attending.

"Where is he?" he said again, "are you concealing him here. I have already been to your office, and he was n't there, and to his flat, and he was n't there."

"Thank God," ejaculated the lawyer.

"By all means if you like. But I 've got to see him, you know. Where is he?"

"He is away in town," said Mr. Taynton, "but he will be back to-night. Now attend. Of course you must see him, I quite understand that. But you must n't see him alone, while you are like this."

"No, I don't want to," said Morris. "I should like other people to see what I 've got to — to say to him — that, that partner of yours."

"He has from this moment ceased to be my partner," said Mr. Taynton brokenly. "I could never again sign what he has signed, or work with him, or — or — except once — see him again. He is coming here by appointment at half-past nine. Suppose that we all meet here. We have both got to see him."

Morris nodded and went toward the door. A sudden spasm of anxiety seemed to seize Mr. Taynton.

"What are you going to do now?" he asked.

"I don't know. Drive to Falmer Park perhaps, and tell Sir Richard you cannot see him immediately. Will you see him to-morrow?"

"Yes, I will call to-morrow morning. Morris, promise me you will do nothing rash, nothing that will bring sorrow on all those who love you."

"I shall bring a little sorrow on a man who hates me," said he.

He went out, and Mr. Taynton sat down again, his mouth compressed into hard lines, his forehead heavily frowning. He could not permanently prevent Morris from meeting Godfrey Mills, besides, it was his right to do so, yet how fraught with awful risks to himself that meeting would be! Morris might easily make a violent, even a murderous, assault on the man, but Mills was an expert boxer and wrestler, science would probably get the upper hand of blind rage. But how deadly a weapon Mills had in store against himself; he would certainly tell Morris that if one partner had slandered him the other, whom he so trusted and revered, had robbed him; he would say, too, that Taynton had been cognizant of, and had approved, his slanders. There was no end to the ruin that would certainly be brought about his head if they met. Mills's train, too, would have left London by now; there was no chance of stopping him. Then there was another danger he had not foreseen, and it was too late to stop that now. Morris was going again to Falmer Park, had indeed started, and that afternoon Godfrey Mills would get out of the train, as he had planned, at the station just below, and walk back over the downs to Brighton. What if they met there, alone?"

For an hour perhaps Mr. Taynton delved at these problems, and at the end even it did not seem as if he had solved them satisfactorily, for when he went out of his house, as he did at the end of this time to get a little breeze if such was obtainable, his face was still shadowed and over-clouded. Overclouded too was the sky, and as he stepped out into the street from his garden-room the hot air struck him like a buffet; and in his troubled and apprehensive mood it felt as if some hot hand warned him by a blow not to venture out of his house. But the house, somehow, in the last hour had become terrible to him, any movement or action, even on a day like this, when only madmen and the English go abroad, was better than the nervous waiting in his dark-ened room. Dreadful forces, forces of ruin and murder and disgrace, were abroad in the world of men; the menace of the low black clouds and stifling heat was more bearable. He wanted to get away from his house, which was permeated and soaked in association with the other two actors, who in company with himself, had surely some tragedy for which the curtain was already rung up. Some dreadful scene was already prepared for them; the setting and stage were ready, the prompter, and who was he? was in the box ready to tell them the next line if any of them faltered. The prompter, surely he was destiny, fate, the irresistible course of events, with which no man can struggle, any more than the actor can struggle with or alter the lines that are set down for him. He may mumble them, he may act dispiritedly and tamely, but he has undertaken a certain part; he has to go through with it.

Though it was a populous hour of the day, there were but few people abroad when Mr. Taynton came out to the sea front; a few cabs stood by the railings that bounded the broad asphalt path which faced the sea, but the drivers of these, despairing of fares, were for the most part dozing on the boxes, or with a more set purpose were frankly slumbering in the interior. The dismal little wooden shelters that punctuated the parade were deserted, the pier stretched an untenanted length of boards over the still, lead-coloured sea, and it seemed as if nature herself was waiting for some elemental catastrophe.

And though the afternoon was of such hideous and sultry heat, Mr. Taynton, though he walked somewhat more briskly than his wont, was conscious of no genial heat that produced perspiration, and the natural reaction and cooling of the skin. Some internal excitement and fever of the brain cut off all external things; the loneliness, the want of correspondence that fever brings between external and internal conditions, was on him. At one moment, in spite of the heat, he shivered, at another he felt that an apoplexy must strike him.

For some half hour he walked to and fro along the sea-wall, between the blackness of the sky and the lead-coloured water, and then his thoughts turned to the downs above this stricken place, where, even in the sultriest days some breath of wind was always moving. Just opposite him, on the other side of the road, was the street that led steeply upward to the station. He went up it.

It was about half-past seven o'clock that evening that the storm burst. A few huge drops of rain fell on the hot pavements, then the rain ceased again, and the big splashes dried, as if the stones had been blotting paper that sucked the moisture in. Then without other warning a streamer of fire split the steeple of St. Agnes's Church, just opposite Mr. Taynton's house, and the crash of thunder answered it more quickly than his servant had run to open the door to Morris's furious ringing of the bell. At that the sluices of heaven were opened, and heaven's artillery thundered its salvoes to the flare of the reckless storm.   In the next half-hour a dozen houses in Brighton were struck, while the choked gutters overflowing on to the streets made ravines and waterways down the roadways. Then the thunder and lightning ceased, but the rain still poured down relentlessly and windlessly, a flood of perpendicular water.

Mr. Taynton had gone out without umbrella, and when he let himself in by his latch-key at his own house-door about half-past eight, it was no wonder that he wrung out his coat and trousers so that he should not soak his Persian rugs.   But from him, as from the charged skies, some tension

had passed; this tempest which had
so cooled the air and restored the
equilibrium of its forces had smoothed
the frowning creases of his brow, and
when the servant hurried up at the
sound of the banged front-door, he
found his master soaked indeed, but
serene.

"Yes, I got caught by the storm,
Williams," he said, "and I am
drenched. The lightning was terrific,
was it not? I will just change, and
have a little supper; some cold meat,
anything that there is. Yes, you
might take my coat at once."

He divested himself of this.

"And I expect Mr. Morris this
evening," he said. "He will probably
have dined, but if not I am sure Mrs.
Otter will toss up a hot dish for him.
Oh, yes, and Mr. Mills will be here at
half-past nine, or even sooner, as I
cannot think he will have walked from
Falmer as he intended. But whenever

he comes, I will see him. He has not been here already?"

"No, sir," said Williams, "Will you have a hot bath, sir?"

"No, I will just change. How battered the poor garden will look to-morrow after this deluge."

Mr. Taynton changed his wet clothes and half an hour afterwards he sat down to his simple and excellent supper. Mrs. Otter had provided an admirable vegetable soup for him, and some cold lamb with asparagus and endive salad. A macedoine of strawberries followed and a scoop of cheese. Simple as his fare was, it just suited Mr. Taynton's tastes, and he was indulging himself with the rather rare luxury of a third glass of port when Williams entered again.

"Mr. Assheton," he said, and held the door open.

Morris came in; he was dressed in

evening clothes with a dinner jacket, and gave no salutation to his host.

"He's not come yet?" he asked.

But his host sprang up.

"Dear boy," he said, "what a relief it is to see you. Ever since you left this afternoon I have had you on my mind. You will have a glass of port?"

Morris laughed, a curious jangling laugh.

"Oh yes, to drink his health," he said.

He sat down with a jerk, and leaned his elbows on the table.

"He'll want a lot of health to carry him through this, won't he?" he asked.

He drank his glass of port like water, and Mr. Taynton instantly filled it up again for him.

"Ah, I remember you don't like port," he said. "What else can I offer you?"

"Oh, this will do very well," said Morris. "I am so thirsty."

"You have dined?" asked his host quietly.

"No; I don't think I did. I was n't hungry."

The Cromwellian clock chimed a remnant half hour.

"Half-past," said Morris, filling his glass again. "You expect him then, don't you?"

"Mills is not always very punctual," said Mr. Taynton.

For the next quarter of an hour the two sat with hardly the interchange of a word. From outside came the swift steady hiss of the rain on to the shrubs in the garden, and again the clock chimed. Morris who at first had sat very quiet had begun to fidget and stir in his chair; occasionally when he happened to notice it, he drank off the port with which Mr. Taynton hospitably kept his glass supplied. Sometimes he relit a cigarette only to let it go out again. But when the clock struck he got up.

"I wonder what has happened," he said. "Can he have missed his train? What time ought he to have got in?"

"He was to have got to Falmer," said Mr. Taynton with a little emphasis on the last word, "at a quarter to seven. He spoke of walking from there."

Morris looked at him with a furtive sidelong glance.

"Why, I — I might have met him there," he said. "I went up there again after I left you to tell Sir Richard you would call to-morrow."

"You saw nothing of him?" asked the lawyer.

"No, of course not. Otherwise — There was scarcely a soul on the road; the storm was coming up. But he would go by the downs, would he not?"

"The path over the downs does n't branch off for a quarter of a mile below Falmer station," said Mr. Taynton.

The minutes ticked on till ten. Then Morris went to the door.

"I shall go round to his rooms to see if he is there," he said.

"There is no need," said his host, "I will telephone."

The instrument hung in a corner of the room, and with very little delay, Mills's servant was rung up. His master had not yet returned, but he had said that he should very likely be late.

"And he made an appointment with you for half-past nine?" asked Morris again.

"Yes. I cannot think what has happened to detain him."

Morris went quickly to the door again.

"I believe it is all a trick," he said, "and you don't want me to meet him. I believe he is in his rooms the whole time. I shall go and see."

Before Mr. Taynton could stop him he had opened the front-door and banged it behind him, and was off hatless and coatless through the pouring perpendicular rain.

Mr. Taynton ran to the door, as if to stop him, but Morris was already halfway down the street, and he went upstairs to the drawing-room. Morris was altogether unlike himself; this discovery of Mills's treachery seemed to have changed his nature. Violent and quick he always was, but to-night he was suspicious, he seemed to distrust Mr. Taynton himself. And, a thing which his host had never known him do before, he had drunk in that half hour when they sat waiting, close on a bottle of port.

The evening paper lay ready cut for him in its accustomed place, but for some five minutes Mr. Taynton did not appear to notice it, though evening papers, on the money-market page, might contain news so frightfully momentous to him. But something, this strangeness in Morris, no doubt, and his general anxiety and suspense as to how this dreadful knot could unravel itself, preoccupied him now, and even when he did take up the paper and turn to the reports of Stock Exchange dealings, he was conscious of no more than a sort of subaqueous thrill of satisfaction. For Boston Copper had gone up nearly a point since the closing price of last night.

It was not many minutes, however before Morris returned with matted and streaming hair and drenched clothes.

"He has not come back," he said. "I went to his rooms and satisfied myself of that, though I think they thought I was mad. I searched them you understand; I insisted. I shall go round there again first thing to-morrow morning, and if he is not there, I shall go up to find him in town. I can't wait; I simply can't wait."

Mr. Taynton looked at him gravely, then nodded.

"No, I guess how you are feeling," he said, "I cannot understand what has happened to Mills; I hope nothing is wrong. And now, my dear boy, let me implore you to go straight home, get off your wet things and go to bed. You will pay heavily for your excitement, if you are not careful."

"I 'll get it out of him." said Morris.

## CHAPTER VI

MORRIS, as Mr. Taynton had advised, though not because he advised it, had gone straight home to the house in Sussex Square, had stripped off his dripping clothes, and then, since this was the line of least resistance, had gone to bed. He did not feel tired, and he longed with that aching longing of the son for the mother, that Mrs. Assheton had been here, so that he could just be in her presence, and, if he found himself unable to speak and tell her all the hideous happenings of those last days, let her presence bring a sort of healing to his tortured mind. But though he was conscious of no tiredness, he was tired to the point of exhaustion, and he had hardly got into bed, when he fell fast asleep. Outside, hushing him to rest, there sounded the sibilant rain, and from the sea below ripples broke gently and rhythmically on the pebbly beach. Nature, too, it seemed, was exhausted by that convulsion of the elements that had turned the evening into a clamorous hell of fire and riot, and now from very weariness she was weeping herself asleep.

It was not yet eleven when Morris had got home, and he slept dreamlessly with that recuperative sleep of youth for some six hours. Then, as within the secret economy of the brain the refreshment of slumber repaired the exhaustion of the day before, he began to dream with strange lurid distinctness, a sort of resurrection dream of which the events of the two days before supplied the bones and skeleton outline. As in all very vivid and dreadful dreams the whole vision was connected and coherent, there were

no ludicrous and inconsequent inter-
ludes, none of those breakings of one
thread and hurried seizures of another,
which though one is dreaming very
distinctly, supply some vague mental
comfort, since even to the sleeper
they are reminders that his experiences
are not solid but mere phantasies
woven by imperfect consciousness and
incomplete control of thought. It was
not thus that Morris dreamed; his
dream was of the solid and sober
texture of life.

He was driving in his motor, he
thought, down the road from the house
at Falmer Park, which through the
gate of a disused lodge joins the main
road, that leads from Falmer Station
to Brighton. He had just heard from
Sir Richard's own lips who it was who
had slandered and blackened him, but,
in his dream, he was conscious of no
anger. The case had been referred to
some higher power, some august court

of supreme authority, which would certainly use its own instruments for its own vengeance. He felt he was concerned in the affair no longer; he was but a spectator of what would be. And, in obedience to some inward dictation, he drove his motor on to the grass behind the lodge, so that it was concealed from the road outside, and walked along the inside of the park-palings, which ran parallel with it.

The afternoon, it seemed, was very dark, though the atmosphere was extraordinarily clear, and after walking along the springy grass inside the railings for some three hundred yards, where was the southeastern corner of the park enclosure, he stopped at the angle and standing on tip-toe peered over them, for they were nearly six feet high, and looked into the road below. It ran straight as a billiard-cue just here, and was visible for a long distance, but at the corner, just outside the palings, the footpath over the downs to Brighton left the road, and struck upward. On the other side of the road ran the railway, and in this clear dark air, Morris could see with great distinctness Falmer Station some four hundred yards away, a a long stretch of the line on the other side of it.

As he looked he saw a puff of steam rise against the woods beyond the station, and before long a train, going Brightonward, clashed into the station. Only one passenger got out, and he came out of the station into the road. He was quite recognisable even at this distance. In his dream Morris felt that he expected to see him get out of the train, and walk along the road; the whole thing seemed pre-ordained. But he ceased tiptoeing to look over the paling; he could hear the passenger's steps when he came nearer.

He thought he waited quietly, squatting down on the mossy grass behind the paling. Something in his hands seemed angry, for his fingers kept tearing up the short turf, and the juice of the severed stems was red like blood. Then in the gathering darkness he heard the tip-tap of footsteps on the highway. But it never occurred to him that this passenger would continue on the highroad; he was certainly going over the downs to Brighton.

The air was quite windless, but at this moment Morris heard the boughs of the oak-tree immediately above him stir and shake, and looking up he saw Mr. Taynton sitting in a fork of the tree. That, too, was perfectly natural; Mr. Taynton was Mills's partner; he was there as a sort of umpire. He held a glass of port wine in one hand, and was sipping it in a leisurely manner, and when Morris looked up

at him, he smiled at him, but put his
finger to his lips, as if recommending
silence. And as the steps on the road
outside sounded close he turned a
meaning glance in the direction of the
road. From where he sat high in the
tree, it was plain to Morris that he
must command the sight of the road,
and was, in his friendly manner,
directing operations.

Suddenly the sound of the steps
ceased, and Morris wondered for the
moment whether Mills had stopped.
But looking up again, he saw Mr.
Taynton's head twisted round to the
right, still looking over the palings.
But Morris found at once that the
footsteps were noiseless, not because
the walker had paused, but because
they were inaudible on the grass. He
had left the road, as the dreamer felt
certain he would, and was going over
the downs to Brighton. At that Morris got up, and still inside the park,

railings followed in the direction he had gone. Then for the first time in his dream, he felt angry, and the anger grew to rage, and the rage to quivering madness. Next moment he had vaulted the fence, and sprang upon the walker from behind. He dealt him blows with some hard instrument, belabouring his head, while with his left hand he throttled his throat so that he could not scream. Only a few were necessary, for he knew that each blow went home, since all the savage youthful strength of shoulder and loose elbow directed them. Then he withdrew his left hand from the throttled throat of the victim who had ceased to struggle, and like a log he fell back on to the grass, and Morris for the first time looked on his face. It was not Mills at all; it was Mr. Taynton.

The terror plucked him from his

sleep; for a moment he wrestled and struggled to raise his head from the pillow and loosen the clutch of the night-hag who had suddenly seized him, and with choking throat and streaming brow he sat up in bed. Even then his dream was more real to him than the sight of his own familiar room, more real than the touch of sheet and blanket or the dew of anguish which his own hand wiped from his forehead and throat. Yet, what was his dream? Was it merely some subconscious stringing together of suggestions and desires and events vivified in sleep to a coherent story (all but that recognition of Mr. Taynton, which was nightmare pure and simple), or *had it happened?*

With waking, anyhow, the public life, the life that concerned other living folk as well as himself, became predominant again. He had certainly seen Sir Richard the day before, and

Sir Richard had given him the name of the man who had slandered him. He had gone to meet that man, but he had not kept his appointment, nor had he come back to his flat in Brighton. So to-day he, Morris, was going to call there once more, and if he did not find him, was going to drive up to London, and seek him there.

But he had been effectually plucked from further sleep, sleep had been strangled, and he got out of bed and went to the window. Nature, in any case, had swept her trouble away, and the pure sweet morning was beginning to dawn in lines of yellow and fleeces of rosy cloud on the eastern horizon.

All that riot and hurly-burly of thunder, the bull's eye flashing of lightning, the perpendicular rain were things of the past, and this morning a sky of pale limpid blue, flecked only by the thinnest clouds, stretched from horizon to horizon. Below the mirror of the sea seemed as deep and as placid as the sky above it, and the inimitable freshness of the dawn spoke of a world rejuvenated and renewed.

It was, by his watch, scarcely five; in an hour it would be reasonable to call at Mills's flat, and see if he had come by the midnight train. If not his motor could be round by soon after six, and he would be in town by eight, before Mills, if he had slept there, would be thinking of starting for Brighton. He was sure to catch him.

Morris had drawn up the blind, and through the open window came the cool breath of the morning ruffling his hair, and blowing his night-shirt close to his skin, and just for that moment, so exquisite was this feeling of renewal and cleanness in the hour of dawn, he thought with a sort of incredulous wonder of the red murderous hate which had possessed him the evening before. He seemed to have been literally beside himself with anger and his words, his thoughts, his actions had been controlled by a force and a possession which was outside himself. Also the dreadful reality of his dream still a little unnerved him, and though he was himself now and awake, he felt that he had been no less himself when he throttled the throat of that abhorred figure that walked up the noiseless path over the downs to Brighton, and with vehement and savage blows clubbed it down. And then the shock of finding it was his old friend whom he had done to death! That, it is true, was nightmare pure and simple, but all the rest was clad in sober, convincing garb of events that had really taken place. He could not at once separate his dream from reality, for indeed what had he done yesterday after he had learned who his traducer had been? He scarcely knew; all events and facts seemed colourless compared to the rage and mad lust for vengeance which had occupied his entire consciousness.

Thus, as he dressed, the thoughts and the rage of yesterday began to stir and move in his mind again. His hate and his desire that justice should be done, that satisfaction should be granted him, was still in his heart. But now they were not wild and flashing flames; they burned with a hard, cold, even light. They were already part of himself, integral pieces and features of his soul. And the calm beauty and peace of the morning ceased to touch him, he had a stern piece of business to put through before he could think of anything else.

It was not yet six when he arrived at the house in which was Mills's flat. A few housemaids were about, but the lift was not yet working, and

he ran upstairs and rang at the bell.
It was answered almost immediately,
for Mills's servant supposed it must be
his master arriving at this early hour,
since no one else would come then,
and he opened the door, half dressed,
with coat and trousers only put over
his night things.

"Is Mr. Mills back yet?" asked
Morris.

"No, sir."

Morris turned to go, but then
stopped, his mind still half-suspicious
that he had been warned by his
partner, and was lying *perdu*.

"I'll give you another ten shillings,"
he said, "if you'll let me come in and
satisfy myself."

The man hesitated.

"A sovereign," said Morris.

He went back to Sussex Square after
this, roused Martin, ordering him to
bring the motor round at once, and

drank a cup of tea, for he would breakfast in town. His mother he expected
would be back during the morning,
and at the thought of her he remembered that this was June 24th, her
birthday, and that his present to her
would be arriving by the early post.
He gave orders, therefore, that a packet
for him from Asprey's was not to be
unpacked, but given to her on her
arrival with her letters. A quarter
of an hour later he was off, leaving
Martin behind, since there were various
businesses in the town which he wanted
him to attend to.

Mr. Taynton, though an earlier riser
than his partner, considered that half
past nine was soon enough to begin
the day, and punctually at that time he
came downstairs to read, as his custom
was, a few collects and some short
piece of the Bible to his servants,
before having his breakfast. That

little ceremony over he walked for a few minutes in his garden while Williams brought in his toast and tea-urn, and observed that though the flowers would no doubt be all the better for the liberal watering of the day before, it was idle to deny that the rain had not considerably damaged them. But his attention was turned from these things to Williams who told him that breakfast was ready, and also brought him a telegram. It was from Morris, and had been sent off from the Sloane Square office an hour before.

Mills is not in town; they say he left yesterday afternoon. Please inform me if you know whether this is so, or if you are keeping him from me. Am delayed by break-down. Shall be back about five.— MORRIS, Bachelors' Club.

Mr. Taynton read this through twice, as is the habit of most people with telegrams, and sent, of course, the reply that all he knew was that his

partner intended to come back last
night, since he had made an appointment with him. Should he arrive
during the day he would telegraph.
He himself was keeping nothing from
Morris, and had not had any correspondence or communication with his
partner since he had left Brighton for
town three days before.

The telegram was a long one, but
Mr. Taynton still sat with poised pen.
Then he added, "Pray do nothing
violent, I implore you." And he
signed it.

He sat rather unusually long over
his breakfast this morning, though he
ate but little, and from the cheerful
smiling aspect of his face it would
seem that his thoughts were pleasant
to him. He was certainly glad that
Morris had not yet come across Mills,
for he trusted that the lapse of a day
or two would speedily calm down the

lad's perfectly justifiable indignation. Besides, he was in love, and his suit had prospered; surely there were pleasanter things than revenge to occupy him. Then his face grew grave a moment as he thought of Morris's mad, murderous outburst of the evening before, but that gravity was short-lived, and he turned with a sense of pleasant expectation to see recorded again the activity and strength of Boston Coppers. But the reality was far beyond his expectations; copper had been strong all day, and in the street afterward there had been renewed buying from quarters which were usually well informed. Bostons had been much in request, and after hours they had had a further spurt, closing at £7 10s. Already in these three days he had cleared his option, and at present prices the shares showed a profit of a point. Mills would have to acknowledge that his perspicacity had been at fault, when he distrusted this last purchase.

He left his house at about half-past ten, and again immured himself in the birdcage lift that carried him up to his partner's flat, where he inquired if he had yet returned. Learning he had not, he asked to be given pen and paper, to write a note for him, which was to be given to him on his arrival.

DEAR MILLS,

Mr. Morris Assheton has learned that you have made grave accusations about him to Sir Richard Templeton, Bart. That you have done so appears to be beyond doubt, and it of course rests with you to substantiate them. I cannot of course at present believe that you could have done so without conclusive evidence; on the other hand I cannot believe that Mr. Assheton is of the character which you have given him.

I therefore refrain, as far as I am able,

from drawing any conclusion till the matter is cleared up.

I may add that he deeply resents your conduct; his anger and indignation were terrible to see.

Sincerely yours,

EDWARD TAYNTON.

GODFREY MILLS, ESQ.

Mr. Taynton read this through, and glanced round, as if to see whether the servants had left the room. Then he sat with closed eyes for a moment, and took an envelope, and swiftly addressed it. He smudged it, however, in blotting it, and so crumpled it up, threw it into the waste-paper basket. He then addressed a second one, and into this he inserted his letter, and got up.

The servant was waiting in the little hall outside.

"Please give this to Mr. Mills when he arrives," he said. "You expected him last night, did you not?"

Mr. Taynton found on arrival at his office that, in his partner's absence, there was a somewhat heavy day of work before him, and foresaw that he would be occupied all afternoon and indeed probably up to dinner time. But he was able to get out for an hour at half-past twelve, at which time, if the weather was hot, he generally indulged in a swim. But to-day there was a certain chill in the air after yesterday's storm, and instead of taking his dip, he walked along the sea front toward Sussex Square. For in his warm-hearted way, seeing that Morris was, as he had said, to tell his mother to-day about his happy and thoroughly suitable love affair, Mr. Taynton proposed to give a little *partie carrée* on the earliest possible evening, at which the two young lovers, Mrs. Assheton, and him-self would form the table. He would learn from her what was the earliest night on which she and Morris were disengaged, and then write to that delightful girl whose affections dear Morris had captured.

But at the corner of the square, just as he was turning into it, there bowled swiftly out a victoria drawn by two horses; he recognised the equipage, he recognised also Mrs. Assheton who was sitting in it. Her head, however, was turned the other way, and Mr. Taynton's hand, already half-way up to his hat was spared the trouble of journeying farther.

But he went on to the house, since his invitation could be easily conveyed by a note which he would scribble there, and was admitted by Martin. Mrs. Assheton, however, was out, a fact which he learned with regret, but, if he might write a note to her, his walk would not be wasted. Accordingly he was shown up into the drawing-room, where on the writing-table was laid an open blotting-book. Even in so small a detail as a blotting-book the careful appointment of the house was evident, for the blotting-paper was absolutely clean and white, a virgin field.

Mr. Taynton took up a quill pen, thought over for a moment the wording of his note and then wrote rapidly. A single side of notepaper was sufficient; he blotted it on the pad, and read it through. But something in it, it must be supposed, did not satisfy him, for he crumpled it up. Ah, at last and for the first time there was a flaw in the appointment of the house, for there was no waste-paper basket by the table. At any rate one must suppose that Mr. Taynton did not see it, for he put his rejected sheet into his pocket.

He took another sheet of paper, selecting from the various stationery that stood in the case a plain piece, rejecting that which was marked with the address of the house, wrote his own address at the head, and proceeded for the second time to write his note of invitation.

But first he changed the quill for his own stylograph, and wrote with that. This was soon written, and by the time he had read it through it was dry, and did not require to be blotted. He placed it in a plain envelope, directed it, and with it in his hand left the room, and went briskly downstairs.

Martin was standing in the hall.

"I want this given to Mrs. Assheton when she comes in, Martin," he said.

He looked round, as he had done once before when speaking to the boy.

"I left it at the door," he said with quiet emphasis. "Can you remember that? I left it. And I hope, Martin, that you have made a fresh start, and that I need never be obliged to tell anybody what I know about you. You will remember my instructions?

I left this at the door. Thank you. My hat? Yes, and my stick."

Mr. Taynton went straight back to his office, and though this morning there had seemed to him to be a good deal of work to be got through, he found that much of it could be delegated to his clerks. So before leaving to go to his lunch, he called in Mr. Timmins.

"Mr. Mills not been here all morning?" he asked. "No? Well, Timmins, there is this packet which I want him to look at, if he comes in before I am back. I shall be here again by five, as there is an hour's work for me to do before evening. Yes, that is all, thanks. Please tell Mr. Mills I shall come back, as I said. How pleasant this freshness is after the rain. The 'clear shining after rain.' Wonderful words! Yes, Mr. Timmins, you will find the verse in the second book of Samuel and the twenty-third chapter."

# CHAPTER VII

MR. TAYNTON made but a short meal of lunch, and ate but sparingly, for he meant to take a good walk this afternoon, and it was not yet two o'clock when he came out of his house again, stick in hand. It was a large heavy stick that he carried, a veritable club, one that it would be easy to recognise amid a host of others, even as he had recognised it that morning in the rather populous umbrella-stand in the hall of Mrs. Assheton's house. He had, it may be remembered, more office work to get through before evening, so he prepared to walk out as far as the limits of the time at his disposal would admit and take the train back. And since there could be nothing more pleasur-

able in the way of walking than
locomotion over the springy grass of
the downs, he took, as he had done a
hundred times before, the road that
led to Falmer.  A hundred yards out
of Brighton there was a stile by the
roadside; from there a footpath, if it
could be dignified by the name of
path at all, led over the hills to a
corner of Falmer Park.  From there
three or four hundred yards of highway would bring him to the station.
He would be in good time to catch the
4.30 train back, and would thus be
at his office again for an hour's work
at five.

His walk was solitary and unevent-
ful, but, to one of so delicate and
sensitive a mind, full of tiny but
memorable sights and sounds.  Up
on these high lands there was a con-
siderable breeze, and Mr. Taynton
paused for a minute or two beside a
windmill that stood alone, in the

expanse of down, watching, with a sort of boyish wonder, the huge flails swing down and aspire again in the circles of their tireless, toil. A little farther on was a grass-grown tumulus of Saxon times, and his mind was distracted from the present to those early days when the unknown dead was committed to this wind-swept tomb. Forests of pine no doubt then grew around his resting place, it was beneath the gloom and murmur of their sable foliage that this dead chief was entrusted to the keeping of the kindly earth. He passed, too, over the lines of a Roman camp; once this sunny empty down re-echoed to the clang of arms, the voices of the living were mingled with the cries and groans of the dying, for without doubt this stronghold of Roman arms was not won, standing, as it did, on the topmost commanding slope of the hills, without slaughter. Yet to-day the peaceful clumps of cistus and the trembling harebell blossomed on the battlefield.

From this point the ground declined swiftly to the main road. Straight in front of him were the palings of Falmer Park, and the tenantless down with its long smooth curves, was broken up into sudden hillocks and depressions. Dells and dingles, some green with bracken, others half full of water lay to right and left of the path, which, as it approached the corner of the park, was more strongly marked than when it lay over the big open spaces. It was somewhat slippery, too, after the torrent of yesterday, and Mr. Taynton's stick saved him more than once from slipping. But before he got down to the point where the corner of the park abutted on the main road, he had leaned on it too heavily, and for all its seeming strength, it had broken in the middle.

The two pieces were but luggage to him and just as he came to the road, he threw them away into a wooded hollow that adjoined the path. The stick had broken straight across; it was no use to think of having it mended.

He was out of the wind here, and since there was still some ten minutes to spare, he sat down on the grassy edge of the road to smoke a cigarette. The woods of the park basked in the fresh sunshine; three hundred yards away was Falmer Station, and beyond that the line was visible for a mile as it ran up the straight valley. Indeed he need hardly move till he saw the steam of his train on the limit of the horizon. That would be ample warning that it was time to go.

Then from far away, he heard the throbbing of a motor, which grew suddenly louder as it turned the corner of the road by the station. It seemed

to him to be going very fast, and
the huge cloud of dust behind it
endorsed his impression.  But almost
immediately after passing this corner
it began to slow down, and the cloud
of dust behind it died away.

At the edge of the road where Mr.
Taynton sat, there were standing several
thick bushes.  He moved a little away
from the road, and took up his seat
again behind one of them.  The car
came very slowly on, and stopped
just opposite him.  On his right lay
the hollow where he had thrown the
useless halves of his stick, on his left
was the corner of the Falmer Park
railings.  He had recognised the driver
of the car, who was alone.

Morris got out when he had stopped
the car, and then spoke aloud, though
to himself.

"Yes, there's the corner," he said,
"there's the path over the downs.
There ——"

Mr. Taynton got up and came toward him.

"My dear fellow," he said, "I have walked out from Brighton on this divine afternoon, and was going to take the train back. But will you give me the pleasure of driving back with you instead?"

Morris looked at him a moment as if he hardly thought he was real.

"Why, of course," he said.

Mr. Taynton was all beams and smiles.

"And you have seen Mills?" he asked. "You have been convinced that he was innocent of the terrible suspicion? Morris, my dear boy, what is the matter?"

Morris had looked at him for a moment with incredulous eyes. Then he had sat down and covered his face with his hands.

"It's nothing," he said at length. "I felt rather faint. I shall be better

in a minute. Of course I 'll drive
you back.''

He sat huddled up with hidden face
for a moment or two. Mr. Taynton
said nothing, but only looked at him.
Then the boy sat up.

"I 'm all right," he said, "it was
just a dream I had last night. No,
I have not seen Mills; they tell me he
left yesterday afternoon for Brighton.
Shall we go?''

For some little distance they went
in silence; then it seemed that Morris
made an effort and spoke.

"Really, I got what they call 'quite
a turn' just now," he said. "I had a
curiously vivid dream last night about
that corner, and you suddenly appeared in my dream quite unexpect-
edly, as you did just now.''

"And what was this dream?" asked
Mr. Taynton, turning up his coat
collar, for the wind of their movement blew rather shrilly on to his neck.

"Oh, nothing particular," said Morris carelessly, "the vividness was concerned with your appearance; that was what startled me."

Then he fell back into the train of thought that had occupied him all the way down from London.

"I believe I was half-mad with rage last night," he said at length, "but this afternoon, I think I am beginning to be sane again. It's true Mills tried to injure me, but he didn't succeed. And as you said last night I have too deep and intense a cause of happiness to give my thoughts and energies to anything so futile as hatred or the desire for revenge. He is punished already. The fact of his having tried to injure me like that was his punishment. Anyhow, I am sick and tired of my anger."

The lawyer did not speak for a moment, and when he did his voice was trembling.

"God bless you, my dear boy," he said gently.

Morris devoted himself for some little time to the guiding of the car.

"And I want you also to leave it all alone," he said after a while. "I don't want you to dissolve your partnership with him, or whatever you call it. I suppose he will guess that you know all about it, so perhaps it would be best if you told him straight out that you do. And then you can, well, make a few well-chosen remarks you know, and drop the whole damned subject forever."

Mr. Taynton seemed much moved.

"I will try," he said, "since you ask it. But Morris, you are more generous than I am."

Morris laughed, his usual boyish high spirits and simplicity were reasserting themselves again.

"Oh, that's all rot," he said. "It's only because it's so fearfully tiring to go on being angry. But I can't help wondering what has happened to the fellow. They told me at his flat in town that he went off with his luggage yesterday afternoon, and gave orders that all letters were to be sent to his Brighton address. You don't think there's anything wrong, do you?"

"My dear fellow, what could be wrong?" asked Mr. Taquta. "He had some business to do at Lewes on his way down, and I make no doubt he slept there, probably forgetting all about his appointment with me. I would wager you that we shall find he is in Brighton when we get in."

"I'll take that," said Morris. "Half a crown."

"No, no, my usual shilling, my usual shilling," laughed the other.

Morris set Mr. Taynton down at his office, and by way of settling their wager at once, waited at the door,

while the other went upstairs to see
if his partner was there. He had not,
however, appeared there that day,
and Mr. Taynton sent a clerk down to
Morris, to ask him to come up, and
they would ring up Mr. Mills's flat on
the telephone.

This was done, and before many
seconds had elapsed they were in
communication. His valet was there,
still waiting for his master's return,
for he had not yet come back. It
appeared that he was getting rather
anxious, for Mr. Taynton reassured him.

"There is not the slightest cause for
any anxiety," were his concluding
words. "I feel convinced he has merely
been detained. Thanks, that's all.
Please let me know as soon as he
returns."

He drew a shilling from his pocket,
and handed it to Morris. But his
face, in spite of his reassuring words,
was a little troubled. You would

have said that though he might not yet
be anxious, he saw that there was
some possibility of his being so, before
very long. Yet he spoke gaily enough.

"And I made so sure I should win,"
he said. "I shall put it down to
unexpected losses, not connected with
business; eh, Mr. Timmins? Or shall
it be charity? It would never do to
put down 'Betting losses.'"

But this was plainly a little forced,
and Morris waited till Mr. Timmins
had gone out.

"And you really meant that?" he
asked. "You are really not anxious?"

"No, I am not anxious," he said, "but
—but I shall be glad when he comes
back. Is that inconsistent? I think
perhaps it is. Well, let us say then that
I am just a shade anxious. But I may
add that I feel sure my anxiety is quite
unnecessary. That defines it for you."

Morris went straight home from

here, and found that his mother had just returned from her afternoon drive. She had found the blotting book waiting for her when she came back that morning, and was delighted with the gift and the loving remembering thought that inspired it.

"But you should n't spend your money on me, my darling," she said to Morris, "though I just love the impulse that made you."

"Oh, very well," said Morris, kissing her, "let 's have the initials changed about then, and let it be M. A. from H. A."

Then his voice grew grave.

"Mother dear, I 've got another birthday present for you. I think — I think you will like it."

She saw at once that he was speaking of no tangible material gift.

"Yes, dear?" she said.

"Madge and me," said Morris. "Just that."

And Mrs. Assheton did like this second present, and though it made her cry a little, her tears were the sweetest that can be shed.

Mother and son dined alone together, and since Morris had determined to forget, to put out of his mind the hideous injury that Mills had attempted to do him, he judged it to be more consistent with this resolve to tell his mother nothing about it, since to mention it to another, even to her, implied that he was not doing his best to bury what he determined should be dead to him. As usual, they played backgammon together, and it was not till Mrs. Assheton rose to go to bed that she remembered Mr. Taynton's note, asking her and Morris to dine with him on their earliest unoccupied day. This, as is the way in the country, happened to be the next evening, and since the last post had already gone out, she asked Morris if Martin might take the note round for her to-night, since it ought to have been answered before.

That, of course, was easily done, and Morris told his servant to call also at the house where Mr. Mills's flat was situated, and ask the porter if he had come home. The note dispatched his mother went to bed, and Morris went down to the billiard room to practise spot-strokes, a form of hazard at which he was singularly inefficient, and wait for news. Little as he knew Mills, and little cause as he had for liking him, he too, like Mr. Taynton, felt vaguely anxious and perturbed, since "disappearances" are necessarily hedged about with mystery and wondering. His own anger and hatred, too, like mists drawn up and dispersed by the sun of love that had dawned on him, had altogether vanished; the attempt against him had, as it turned out, been so futile, and he genuinely wished to have some assurance of the safety of the man, the thought of whom had so blackened his soul only twenty-four hours ago.

His errands took Martin the best part of an hour, and he returned with two notes, one for Mrs. Assheton, the other for Morris. He had been also to the flat and inquired, but there was no news of the missing man.

Morris opened his note, which was from Mr. Taynton.

DEAR MORRIS,

I am delighted that your mother and you can dine to-morrow, and I am telegraphing first thing in the morning to see if Miss Madge will make our fourth. I feel sure that when she knows what my little party is, she will come.

I have been twice round to see if my partner has returned, and find no news of him. It is idle to deny that I am getting anxious, as I cannot conceive what has happened. Should he not be back by to-morrow morning, I shall put the matter into the hands of the police. I trust that my anxieties are unfounded, but the matter is beginning to look strange.

Affectionately yours,
EDWARD TAYNTON.

There is nothing so infectious as anxiety, and it can be conveyed by look or word or letter, and requires no period of incubation. And Morris began to be really anxious also, with a vague disquietude at the sense of there being something wrong.

## CHAPTER VIII

MR. TAYNTON, according to the intention he had expressed, sent round early next morning (the day of the week being Saturday) to his partner's flat, and finding that he was not there, and that no word of any kind had been received from him, went, as he felt himself now bound to do, to the police office, stated what had brought him there, and gave them all information which it was in his power to give.

It was brief enough; his partner had gone up to town on Tuesday last, and, had he followed his plans should have returned to Brighton by Thursday evening, since he had made an appointment to come to Mr. Taynton's house at nine thirty that night.  It had been ascertained too, by — Mr. Taynton hesitated a moment — by Mr. Morris Assheton in London, that he had left his flat in St. James's Court on Thursday afternoon, to go, presumably, to catch the train back to Brighton. He had also left orders that all letters should be forwarded to him at his Brighton address.

Superintendent Figgis, to whom Mr. Taynton made his statement, was in manner slow, stout, and bored, and looked in every way utterly unfitted to find clues to the least mysterious occurences, unearth crime or run down the criminal. He seemed quite incapable of running down anything, and Mr. Taynton had to repeat everything he said in order to be sure that Mr. Figgis got his notes, which he made in a large round hand, with laborious distinctness, correctly written. Having finished them the Superintendent stared at them mournfully for a little while, and asked Mr. Taynton if he had anything more to add.

"I think that is all," said the lawyer. "Ah, one moment. Mr. Mills expressed to me the intention of perhaps getting out at Falmer and walking over the downs to Brighton. But Thursday was the evening on which we had that terrible thunderstorm. I should think it very unlikely that he would have left the train."

Superintendent Figgis appeared to be trying to recollect something.

"Was there a thunderstorm on Thursday?" he asked.

"The most severe I ever remember," said Mr. Taynton.

"It had slipped my memory," said this incompetent agent of justice.

But a little thought enable him to ask a question that bore on the case.

"He travelled then by Lewes and not by the direct route?"

"Presumably. He had a season ticket via Lewes, since our business often took him there. Had he intended to travel by Hayward's Heath," said Mr. Taynton rather laboriously, as if explaining something to a child, "he could not have intended to get out at Falmer."

Mr. Figgis had to think over this, which he did with his mouth open.

"Seeing that the Hayward's Heath line does not pass Falmer," he suggested.

Mr. Taynton drew a sheet of paper toward him and kindly made a rough sketch-map of railway lines.

"And his season ticket went by the Lewes line," he explained.

Superintendent Figgis appeared to understand this after a while. Then he sighed heavily, and changed the subject with rather disconcerting abruptness.

"From my notes I understand that

Mr. Morris Assheton ascertained that the missing individual had left his flat in London on Thursday afternoon," he said.

"Yes, Mr. Assheton is a client of ours, and he wished to see my partner on a business matter. In fact, when Mr. Mills was found not to have returned on Thursday evening, he went up to London next day to see him, since we both supposed he had been detained there."

Mr. Figgis looked once more mournfully at his notes, altered a palpably mistaken "Wednesday" into Thursday, and got up.

"The matter shall be gone into," he said.

Mr. Taynton went straight from here to his office, and for a couple of hours devoted himself to the business of his firm, giving it his whole attention and working perhaps with more speed

than it was usually his to command.
Saturday of course was a half-holiday,
and it was naturally his desire to get
cleared off everything that would
otherwise interrupt the well-earned
repose and security from business affairs
which was to him the proper atmosphere of the seventh, or as he called
it, the first day. This interview with
the accredited representative of the
law also had removed a certain weight
from his mind. He had placed the
matter of his partner's disappearance
in official hands, he had done all he
could do to clear up his absence, and,
in case — but here he pulled himself
up; it was at present most premature
even to look at the possibility of crime
having been committed.

Mr. Taynton was in no way a vain
man, nor was it his habit ever to
review his own conduct, with the
object of contrasting it favourably with
what others might have done under the

circumstances. Yet he could not help being aware that others less kindly than he would have shrugged sarcastic shoulders and said, "probably another blackmailing errand has detained him." For, indeed, Mills had painted himself in very ugly colours in his last interview with him; that horrid hint of blackmail, which still, so to speak, held good, had cast a new light on him. But now Taynton was conscious of no grudge against him; he did not say, "he can look after himself." He was anxious about his continued absence, and had taken the extreme step of calling in the aid of the police, the national guardian of personal safety.

He got away from his office about half-past twelve and in preparation for the little dinner festival of this evening, for Miss Templeton had sent her joyful telegraphic acceptance, went to several shops to order some few little delicacies to grace his plain bachelor table. An ice-pudding, for instance, was outside the orbit, so he feared of his plain though excellent cook, and two little dishes of chocolates and sweets, since he was at the confectioner's, would be appropriate to the taste of his lady guests. Again a floral decoration of the table was indicated, and since the storm of Thursday, there was nothing in his garden worthy of the occasion; thus a visit to the florist's resulted in an order for smilax and roses.

He got home, however, at his usual luncheon hour to find a telegram waiting for him on the Heppelwhite table in the hall. There had been a continued buying of copper shares, and the feature was a sensational rise in Bostons, which during the morning had gone up a clear point.

Mr. Taynton had no need to make calculations; he knew, as a man knows the multiplication table of two, what every fraction of a rise in Bostons meant to him, and this, provided only he had time to sell at once, meant the complete recovery of the losses he had suffered. With those active markets it was still easily possible though it was Saturday, to effect his sale, since there was sure to be long continued business in the Street and he had but to be able to exercise his option at that price, to be quit of that dreadful incubus of anxiety which for the last two years had been a millstone round his neck that had grown mushroom like. The telephone to town, of course, was far the quickest mode of communication, and having given his order he waited ten minutes till the tube babbled and croaked to him again.

There is a saying that things are "too good to be true," but when Mr. Taynton sat down to his lunch that day, he felt that the converse of the proverb was the correcter epigram.

Things could be so good that they must be true, and here, still ringing in his ears was one of them — Morris — it was thus he phrased it to himself — was "paid off," or, in more business-like language, the fortune of which Mr. Taynton was trustee was intact again, and, like a tit-bit for a good child, there was an additional five or six hundred pounds for him who had managed the trust so well. Mr. Taynton could not help feeling somehow that he deserved it; he had increased Morris's fortune since he had charge of it by £10,000. And what a lesson, too, he had had, so gently and painlessly taught him! No one knew better than he how grievously wrong he had got, in gambling with trust money. Yet now it had come right: he had repaired the original wrong; on Monday he would reinvest this capital in those holdings which he had sold, and Morris's

£40,000 (so largely the result of careful
and judicious investment) would certainly stand the scrutiny of any who
could possibly have any cause to
examine his ledgers. Indeed there
would be nothing to see. Two years
ago Mr. Morris Assheton's fortune was
invested in certain railway debentures
and Government stock. It would in a
few days' time be invested there again,
precisely as it had been. Mr. Taynton
had not been dealing in gilt-edged
securities lately, and could not absolutely trust his memory, but he rather
thought that the repurchase could be
made at a somewhat smaller sum than
had been realised by their various
sales dating from two years ago. In
that case there was a little more *sub
rosa* reward for this well-inspired justice, weighed but featherwise against the
overwhelming relief of the knowledge
he could make wrong things right again,
repair his, yes, his scoundrelism.

How futile, too, now, was Mills's threatened blackmail! Mills might, if he chose, proclaim on any convenient housetop, that his partner had gambled with Morris's £40,000 that according to the ledgers was invested in certain railway debentures and other gilt-edged securities. In a few days, any scrutiny might be made of the securities lodged at the County Bank, and assuredly among them would be found those debentures, those gilt-edged securities exactly as they appeared in the ledgers. Yet Mr. Taynton, so kindly is the nature of happiness, contemplated no revengeful step on his partner; he searched his heart and found that no trace of rancour against poor Mills was hoarded there.

Whether happiness makes us good, is a question not yet decided, but it is quite certain that happiness makes us forget that we have been bad, and it seemed to Mr. Taynton, as he sat in his

cool dining-room, and ate his lunch with
a more vivid appetite than had been his
for many months, it seemed that the
man who had gambled with his client's
money was no longer himself; it was
a perfectly different person who had
done that. It was a different man, too,
who, so few days ago had connived at
and applauded the sorry trick which
Mills had tried to play on Morris, when
(so futilely, it is true) he had slandered
him to Sir Richard. Now he felt that
he — this man that to-day sat here —
was incapable of such meannesses.
And, thank God, it was never too late;
from to-day he would lead the honour-
able, upright existence which the world
(apart from his partner) had always
credited him with leading.

He basked in the full sunshine of
these happy and comfortable thoughts,
and even as the sun of midsummer
lingered long on the sea and hills, so

for hours this inward sunshine warmed and cheered him. Nor was it till he saw by his watch that he must return from the long pleasant ramble on which he had started as soon as lunch was over, that a cloud filmy and thin at first began to come across the face of the sun. Once and again those genial beams dispersed it, but soon it seemed as if the vapours were getting the upper hand. A thought, in fact, had crossed Mr. Taynton's mind that quite distinctly dimmed his happiness. But a little reflection told him that a very simple step on his part would put that right again, and he walked home rather more quickly than he had set out, since he had this little bit of business to do before dinner.

He went — this was only natural — to the house where Mr. Mills's flat was situated, and inquired of the porter whether his partner had yet returned. But the same answer as before was

given him, and saying that he had
need of a document that Mills had
taken home with him three days before
he went up in the lift, and rang the
bell of the flat. But it was not his
servant who opened it, but sad Superintendent Figgis.

For some reason this was rather a
shock to Mr. Taynton; to expect one
face and see another is always (though
ever so slightly) upsetting, but he
instantly recovered himself and
explained his errand.

"My partner took home with him
on Tuesday a paper, which is concerned with my business," he said.
"Would you kindly let me look round
or it?"

Mr. Figgis weighed this request.

"Nothing must be removed from the
rooms," he said, "till we have finished
our search."

"Search for what?" asked Mr.
Taynton.

"Any possible clue as to the reason of Mr. Mills's disappearance. But in ten minutes we shall have done, if you care to wait."

"I don't want to remove anything." said the lawyer. "I merely want to consult ——"

At the moment another man in plain clothes came out of the sitting-room. He carried in his hand two or three letters, and a few scraps of crumpled paper. There was an envelope or two among them.

"We have finished, sir," he said to the Superintendent.

Mr. Figgis turned to the lawyer, who was looking rather fixedly at what the other man had in his hand.

"My document may be among those," he said.

Mr. Figgis handed them to him. There were two envelopes, both addressed to the missing man, one bearing his name only, some small torn-up scrap of paper, and three or four private letters.

"Is it among these?" he asked.

Mr. Taynton turned them over.

"No," he said, "it was — it was a large, yes, a large blue paper, official looking."

"No such thing in the flat, sir," said the second man.

"Very annoying," said the lawyer.

An idea seemed slowly to strike Mr. Figgis.

"He may have taken it to London with him," he said. "But will you not look round?"

Mr. Taynton did so. He also looked in the waste-paper basket, but it was empty.

So he went back to make ready to receive his guests, for the little party. But it had got dark; this "document" whatever it was, appeared to trouble him. The simple step he had contemplated had not led him in quite the right direction.

The Superintendent with his colleague went back into the sitting-room on the lawyer's departure, and Mr. Figgis took from his pocket most of his notes.

"I went to the station, Wilkinson," he said, "and in the lost luggage office I found Mr. Mills's bag. It had arrived on Thursday evening. But it seems pretty certain that its owner did not arrive with it."

"Looks as if he did get out at Falmer," said Wilkinson.

Figgis took a long time to consider this.

"It is possible," he said. "It is also possible that he put his luggage into the train in London, and subsequently missed the train himself."

Then together they went through the papers that might conceivably help them. There was a torn-up letter found in his bedroom fireplace, and the crumpled up envelope that belonged to it. They patiently pieced this together, but found nothing of value. The other letters referred only to his engagements in London, none of which were later than Thursday morning. There remained one crumpled up envelope (also from the paper-basket) but no letter that in any way corresponded with it. It was addressed in a rather sprawling, eager, boyish hand.

"No letter of any sort to correspond?" asked Figgis for the second time.

"No."

"I think for the present we will keep it," said he.

The little party at Mr. Taynton's was gay to the point of foolishness, and of them all none was more light-hearted than the host. Morris had asked him in an undertone, on arrival, whether any more had been heard, and learning there was still no news, had dismissed the subject altogether, The sunshine of the day, too, had come back to the lawyer; his usual cheerful serenity was touched with a sort of sympathetic boisterousness, at the huge spirits of the young couple and it was to be recorded that after dinner they played musical chairs and blind-man's buff, with infinite laughter. Never was an elderly solicitor so spontaneously gay; indeed before long it was he who reinfected the others with merriment. But as always, after abandonment to laughter a little reaction followed, and when they went upstairs from his sitting-room where they had been so uproarious, so that it might be made tidy again before Sunday, and sat in the drawing-room overlooking the street, there did come this little reaction. But it was already eleven, and soon Mrs. Assheton rose to go.

The night was hot, and Morris was sitting to cool himself by the open window, leaning his head out to catch the breeze. The street was very empty and quiet, and his motor, in which as a great concession, his mother had consented to be carried, on the promise of his going slow, had already come for them. Then down at the seaward end of the street he heard street-cries, as if some sudden news had come in that sent the vendors of the evening papers out to reap a second harvest that night. He could not, however, catch what it was, and they all went downstairs together.

Madge was going home with them, for she was stopping over the Sunday with Mrs. Assheton, and the two ladies had already got into the car, while Morris was still standing on the pavement with his host.

Then suddenly a newsboy, with a sheaf of papers still hot from the press, came running from the corner of the street just above them, and as he ran he shouted out the news which was already making little groups of people collect and gather in the streets.

Mr. Taynton turned quickly as the words became audible, seized a paper from the boy, giving him the first coin that he found, and ran back into the hall of his house, Morris with him, to beneath the electric light that burned there. The shrill voice of the boy still shouting the news of murder got gradually less loud as he went further down the street.

They read the short paragraph together, and then looked at each other with mute horror in their eyes.

## CHAPTER IX

THE inquest was held at Falmer on the Monday following, when the body was formally identified by Mr. Taynton and Mills's servant, and they both had to give evidence as regards what they knew of the movements of the deceased. This, as a matter of fact, Mr. Taynton had already given to Figgis, and in his examination now he repeated with absolute exactitude what he had said before including again the fact that Morris had gone up to town on Friday morning to try to find him there. On this occasion, however, a few further questions were put to him, eliciting the fact that the business on which Morris wanted to see him was known to Mr. Taynton but could not be by him repeated

since it dealt with confidential transactions between the firm of solicitors
and their client.  The business was,
yes, of the nature of a dispute, but
Mr. Taynton regarded it as certain
that some amicable arrangement would
have been come to, had the interview
taken place.  As it had not, however,
since Morris had not found him at his
flat in town, he could not speak for
certain on this subject.  The dispute
concerned an action of his partner's,
made independently of him.  Had he
been consulted he would have strongly
disapproved of it.

The body, as was made public now,
had been discovered by accident,
though, as has been seen, the probability of Mills having got out at
Falmer had been arrived at by the
police, and Figgis immediately after
his interview with Mr. Taynton on the
Saturday evening had started for
Falmer to make inquiries there, and

had arrived there within a few minutes
of the discovery of the body. A
carpenter of that village had strolled
out about eight o'clock that night
with his two children while supper was
being got ready, and had gone a piece
of the way up the path over the downs,
which left the road at the corner of
Falmer Park. The children were running and playing about, hiding and
seeking each other in the bracken-
filled hollows, and among the trees,
when one of them screamed suddenly,
and a moment afterward they both
came running to their father, saying
that they had come upon a man in one
of these copses, lying on his face and
they were frightened. He had gone
to see what this terrifying person was,
and had found the body. He went
straight back to the village without
touching anything, for it was clear
both from what he saw and from the
crowd of buzzing flies that the man

was dead, and gave information to
the police.   Then within a few minutes
from that, Mr. Figgis had arrived
from Brighton, to find that it was
superfluous to look any further or
inquire any more concerning the
whereabouts of the missing man.   All
that was mortal of him was here, the
head covered with a cloth, and bits of
the fresh summer growth of fern and
frond sticking to his clothing.

After the identification of the body
came evidence medical and otherwise
that seemed to show beyond doubt
the time and manner of his death and
the possible motive of the murderer.
The base of the skull was smashed in,
evidently by some violent blow dealt
from behind with a blunt heavy instrument of some sort, and death had
probably been instantaneous.   In one
of the pockets was a first edition of
an evening paper published in London
on Thursday last, which fixed the

earliest possible time at which the murder had been committed, while in the opinion of the doctor who examined the body late on Saturday night, the man had been dead not less than forty-eight hours. In spite of the very heavy rain which had fallen on Thursday night, there were traces of a pool of blood about mid-way between the clump of bracken where the body was found, and the path over the downs leading from Falmer to Brighton. This, taken in conjunction with the information already given by Mr. Taynton, made it practically certain that the deceased had left London on the Thursday as he had intended to do, and had got out of the train at Falmer, also according to his expressed intention, to walk to Brighton. It would again have been most improbable that he would have started on his walk had the storm already begun. But the train by which his bag was conveyed to Brighton arrived at Falmer at half-past six, the storm did not burst till an hour afterward.  Finally, with regard to possible motive, the murdered man's watch was missing; his pockets also were empty of coin.

This concluded the evidence, and the verdict was brought in without the jury leaving the court, and "wilful murder by person or persons unknown" was recorded.

Mr. Taynton, as was indeed to be expected, had been much affected during the giving of his evidence, and when the inquest was over, he returned to Brighton feeling terribly upset by this sudden tragedy, which had crashed without warning into his life.  It had been so swift and terrible; without sign or preparation this man, whom he had known so long, had been hurled from life and all its vigour into

death. And how utterly now Mr.
Taynton forgave him for that base
attack that he had made on him,
so few days ago; how utterly, too,
he felt sure Morris had forgiven him
for what was perhaps even harder to
forgive. And if they could forgive
trespasses like these, they who were of
human passion and resentments, surely
the reader of all hearts would forgive.
That moment of agony short though
it might have been in actual duration,
when the murderous weapon split
through the bone and scattered the
brain, surely brought punishment and
therefore atonement for the frailties of
a life-time.

Mr. Taynton, on his arrival back at
Brighton that afternoon, devoted a
couple of solitary hours to such
thoughts as these, and others to which
this tragedy naturally gave rise and
then with a supreme effort of will
he determined to think no more on

the subject. It was inevitable that his mind should again and again perhaps for weeks and months to come fall back on these dreadful events, but his will was set on not permitting himself to dwell on them. So, though it was already late in the afternoon, he set forth again from his house about tea-time, to spend a couple of hours at the office. He had sent word to Mr. Timmins that he would probably come in, and begin to get through the arrears caused by his unavoidable absence that morning, and he found his head clerk waiting for him. A few words were of course appropriate, and they were admirably chosen.

"You have seen the result of the inquest, no doubt, Mr. Timmins," he said, "and yet one hardly knows whether one wishes the murderer to be brought to justice. What good does that do, now our friend is dead? So mean and petty a motive too; just for a watch and a few sovereigns. It was money bought at a terrible price, was it not? Poor soul, poor soul; yes, I say that of the murderer. Well, well, we must turn our faces forward, Mr. Timmins; it is no use dwelling on the dreadful irremediable past. The morning's post? Is that it?"

Mr. Timmins ventured sympathy.

"You look terribly worn out, sir," he said. "Would n't it be wiser to leave it till to-morrow? A good night's rest, you know, sir, if you'll excuse my mentioning it."

"No, no, Mr. Timmins, we must get to work again, we must get to work."

Nature, inspired by the spirit and instinct of life, is wonderfully recuperative. Whether earthquake or famine, fire or pestilence has blotted out a thousand lives, those who are left, like ants when their house is disturbed, waste but little time after the damage

has been done in vain lamentations,
but, slaves to the force of life,
begin almost instantly to rebuild
and reconstruct. And what is true
of the community is true also of the
individual, and thus in three days from
this dreadful morning of the inquest,
Mr. Taynton, after attending the funeral
of the murdered man, was very
actively employed, since the branch of
the firm in London, deprived of its
head, required supervision from him.
Others also, who had been brought
near to the tragedy, were occupied
again, and of these Morris in particular
was a fair example of the spirit of
the Life-force. His effort, no doubt,
was in a way easier than that made by
Mr. Taynton, for to be twenty-two years
old and in love should be occupation
sufficient. But he, too, had his bad
hours, when the past rose phantom-
like about him, and he recalled that
evening when his rage had driven him

nearly mad with passion against his
traducer. And by an awful coinci-
dence, his madness had been contem-
poraneous with the slanderer's death.
He must, in fact, have been within a
few hundred yards of the place at
the time the murder was committed,
for he had gone back to Falmer Park
that day, with the message that Mr.
Taynton would call on the morrow, and
had left the place not half an hour
before the breaking of the storm. He
had driven by the corner of the Park,
where the path over the downs left
the main road and within a few
hundred yards of him at that moment,
had been, dead or alive, the man who
had so vilely slandered him. Supposing — it might so easily have happened
— they had met on the road. What
would he have done? Would he have
been able to pass him and not wreaked
his rage on him? He hardly dared
to think of that. But, life and love

were his, and that which might have been was soon dreamlike in comparison of these. Indeed, that dreadful dream which he had had the night after the murder had been committed was no less real than it. The past was all of this texture, and mistlike, it was evaporated in the beams of the day that was his.

Now Brighton is a populous place, and a sunny one, and many people lounge there in the sun all day. But for the next three or four days a few of these loungers lounged somewhat systematically. One lounged in Sussex Square, another lounged in Montpellier Road, one or two others who apparently enjoyed this fresh air but did not care about the town itself, usually went to the station after breakfast, and spent the day in rambling agreeably about the downs. They also frequented the pleasant little village of Falmer, gossiping freely with its rural

inhabitants. Often footmen or gar-
deners from the Park came down to
the village, and acquaintances were
easily ripened in the ale-house. Otherwise there was not much incident
in the village; sometimes a motor drove
by, and one, after an illegally fast progress along the road, very often turned
in at the park gates. But no prosecution
followed; it was clear they were not
agents of the police. Mr. Figgis, also,
frequently came out from Brighton,
and went strolling about too, very
slowly and sadly. He often wandered
in the little copses that bordered the
path over the downs to Brighton,
especially near the place where it joined
the main road a few hundred yards below
Falmer station. Then came a morning when neither he nor any of the
other chance visitors to Falmer were
seen there any more. But the evening
before Mr. Figgis carried back with
him to the train a long thin package

wrapped in brown paper. But on the
morning when these strangers were
seen no more at Falmer, it appeared
that they had not entirely left the
neighbourhood, for instead of one only
being in the neighbourhood of Sussex
Square, there were three of them
there.

Morris had ordered the motor to be
round that morning at eleven, and it
had been at the door some few minutes
before he appeared. Martin had
driven it round from the stables, but
he was in a suit of tweed; it seemed
that he was not going with it. Then
the front door opened, and Morris
appeared as usual in a violent hurry.
One of the strangers was on the pavement close to the house door, looking
with interest at the car. But his
interest in the car ceased when the boy
appeared. And from the railings of
the square garden opposite another
stranger crossed the road, and from

the left behind the car came a third.

"Mr. Morris Assheton?" said the first.

"Well, what then?" asked Morris.

The two others moved a little nearer.

"I arrest you in the King's name," said the first.

Morris was putting on a light coat as he came across the pavement. One arm was in, the other out. He stopped dead; and the bright colour of his face slowly faded, leaving a sort of ashen gray behind. His mouth suddenly went dry, and it was only at the third attempt to speak that words came.

"What for?" he said.

"For the murder of Godfrey Mills," said the man. "Here is the warrant. I warn you that all you say ——"

Morris, whose lithe athletic frame had gone slack for the moment, stiffened himself up again.

"I am not going to say anything,"

he said. "Martin, drive to Mr. Taynton's at once, and tell him that I am arrested."

The other two now had closed round him.

"Oh, I'm not going to bolt," he said. "Please tell me where you are going to take me."

"Police Court in Branksome Street," said the first.

"Tell Mr. Taynton I am there," said Morris to his man.

There was a cab at the corner of the square, and in answer to an almost imperceptible nod from one of the men, it moved up to the house. The square was otherwise nearly empty, and Morris looked round as the cab drew nearer. Upstairs in the house he had just left, was his mother who was coming out to Falmer this evening to dine; above illimitable blue stretched from horizon to horizon, behind was the free fresh sea. Birds chirped in the bushes and lilac was in flower. Everything had its liberty.

Then a new instinct seized him, and though a moment before he had given his word that he was not meditating escape, liberty called to him. Everything else was free. He rushed forward, striking right and left with his arms, then tripped on the edge of the paving stones and fell. He was instantly seized, and next moment was in the cab, and fetters of steel, though he could not remember their having been placed there, were on his wrists.

# CHAPTER X

I T WAS a fortnight later, a hot July
morning, and an unusual anima-
tion reigned in the staid and leisurely
streets of Lewes. For the Assizes
opened that day, and it was known
that the first case to be tried was the
murder of which all Brighton and a
large part of England had been talking
so much since Morris Assheton had
been committed for trial. At the hear-
ing in the police-court there was not
very much evidence brought forward,
but there had been sufficient to make
it necessary that he should stand his
trial. It was known, for instance,
that he had some very serious
reason for anger and resentment
against his victim; those who had seen
him that day remembered him as being

utterly unlike himself; he was known
to have been at Falmer Park that
afternoon about six, and to have
driven home along the Falmer Road
in his car an hour or so later.  And
in a copse close by to where the body of
the murdered man was found had been
discovered a thick bludgeon of a stick,
broken it would seem by some violent
act, into two halves.  On the top half
was rudely cut with a pen-knife
M. ASSHE . . . What was puz-
zling, however, was the apparent
motive of robbery about the crime;
it will be remembered that the victim's
watch was missing, and that no money
was found on him.

But since Morris had been brought
up for committal at the police-court
it was believed that a quantity more
evidence of a peculiarly incriminating
kind had turned up.  Yet in spite
of this, so it was rumoured, the prisoner
apparently did more than bear up;

it was said that he was quite cheerful, quite confident that his innocence would be established. Others said that he was merely callous and utterly without any moral sense. Much sympathy of course was felt for his mother, and even more for the family of the Templetons and the daughter to whom it was said that Morris was actually engaged. And, as much as anyone it was Mr. Taynton who was the recipient of the respectful pity of the British public. Though no relation he had all his life been a father to Morris, and while Miss Madge Templeton was young and had the spring and elasticity of youth, so that, though all this was indeed terrible enough, she might be expected to get over it, Mr. Taynton was advanced in years and it seemed that he was utterly broken by the shock. He had not been in Brighton on the day on which Morris was brought before the police-court magistrates, and the news had reached him in London after his young friend had been committed. It was said he had fainted straight off, and there had been much difficulty in bringing him round. But since then he had worked day and night on behalf of the accused. But certain fresh evidence which had turned up a day or two before the Assizes seemed to have taken the heart out of him. He had felt confident that the watch would have been found, and the thief traced. But something new that had turned up had utterly staggered him. He could only cling to one hope, and that was that he knew the evidence about the stick must break down, for it was he who had thrown the fragments into the bushes, a fact which would come to light in his own evidence. But at the most, all he could hope for was, that though it seemed as if the poor lad must be condemned, the jury, on account of his youth, and the provocation he had received, of which Mr. Taynton would certainly make the most when called upon to bear witness on this point, or owing to some weakness in the terrible chain of evidence that had been woven, would recommend him to mercy.

The awful formalities at the opening of the case were gone through. The judge took his seat, and laid on the bench in front of him a small parcel wrapped up in tissue paper; the jury was sworn in, and the prisoner asked if he objected to the inclusion of any of those among the men who were going to decide whether he was worthy of life or guilty of death, and the packed court, composed about equally of men and women, most of whom would have shuddered to see a dog beaten, or a tired hare made to go an extra mile, settled themselves in their places with a rustle of satisfaction at the thought of seeing a man brought before them in the shame of suspected murder, and promised themselves an interesting and thrilling couple of days in observing the gallows march nearer him, and in watching his mental agony. They who would, and perhaps did, subscribe to benevolent institutions for the relief of suffering among the lower animals, would willingly have paid a far higher rate to observe the suffering of a man. He was so interesting; he was so young and good-looking; what a depraved monster he must be. And that little package in tissue paper which the judge brought in and laid on the bench! The black cap, was it not? That showed what the judge thought about it all. How thrilling!

Counsel for the Crown, opened the case, and in a speech grimly devoid of all emotional appeal, laid before the court the facts he was prepared to prove, on which they would base their verdict.

The prisoner, a young man of birth and breeding, had, strong grounds for revenge on the murdered man. The prosecution, however, was not concerned in defending what the murdered man had done, but in establishing the guilt of the man who had murdered him. Godfrey Mills, had, as could be proved by witnesses, slandered the prisoner in an abominable manner, and the prosecution were not intending for a moment to attempt to establish the truth of his slander. But this slander they put forward as a motive that gave rise to a murderous impulse on the part of the prisoner. The jury would hear from one of the witnesses, an old friend of the prisoner's, and a man who had been a sort of father to him, that a few hours only before the murder was committed the prisoner had uttered certain words which admitted only of one interpretation, namely that murder was in his mind. That the provocation was great was not denied; it was certain however, that the provocation was sufficient.

Counsel then sketched the actual circumstances of the crime, as far as they could be constructed from what evidence there was. This evidence was purely circumstantial, but of a sort which left no reasonable doubt that the murder had been committed by the prisoner in the manner suggested. Mr. Godfrey Mills had gone to London on the Tuesday of the fatal week, intending to return on the Thursday. On the Wednesday the prisoner became cognisant of the fact that Mr. Godfrey Mills had — he would not argue over it — wantonly slandered him to Sir Richard Templeton, a marriage with the daughter of whom was projected in the prisoner's mind, which there was reason to suppose, might have taken place. Should the jury not be satisfied on that point, witnesses would be called, including the young lady herself, but unless the counsel for the defence challenged their statement, namely that this slander had been spoken which contributed, so it was argued, a motive for the crime it would be unnecessary to intrude on the poignant and private grief of persons so situated, and to insist on a scene which must prove to be so heart-rendingly painful.

(There was a slight movement of demur in the humane and crowded court at this; it was just these heart-rendingly painful things which were so thrilling.)

It was most important, continued counsel for the prosecution that the jury should fix these dates accurately in their minds. Tuesday was June 21st; it was on that day the murdered man had gone to London, designing to return on June 23d, Thursday. The prisoner had learned on Wednesday (June 22d) that aspersions had been made, false aspersions, on his character, and it was on Thursday that he learned for certain from the lips of the man to whom they had been made, who was the author of them. The author was Mr. Godfrey Mills. He had thereupon motored back from Falmer Park, and informed Mr. Taynton of this, and had left again for Falmer an hour later to make an appointment for Mr. Taynton to see Sir Richard. He knew, too, this would be proved, that Mr. Godfrey Mills proposed to return from London that afternoon, to get out at Falmer station and walk back to Brighton. It was certain from the finding of the body that Mr. Mills had travelled from London, as he intended, and that he had got out at this station. It was certain also that at that hour the prisoner, burning for vengeance, and knowing the movements

of Mr. Mills, was in the vicinity of
Falmer.

To proceed, it was certain also that
the prisoner in a very strange wild
state had arrived at Mr. Taynton's
house about nine that evening, knowing that Mr. Mills was expected there
at about 9.30. Granted that he had
committed the murder, this proceed-
ing was dictated by the most elemen-
tary instinct of self-preservation. It was
also in accordance with that that he had
gone round in the pelting rain late that
night to see if the missing man had
returned to his flat, and that he had
gone to London next morning to seek
him there. He had not, of course,
found him, and he returned to Brighton
that afternoon. In connection with
this return, another painful passage
lay before them, for it would be shown
by one of the witnesses that again
on the Friday afternoon the prisoner
had visited the scene of the crime.

Mr. Taynton, in fact, still unsuspicious
of anything being wrong had walked
over the Downs that afternoon from
Brighton to Falmer, and had sat down
in view of the station where he proposed to catch a train back to Brighton,
and had seen the prisoner stop his
motor-car close to the corner where
the body had been found, and behave
in a manner inexplicable except on
the theory that he knew where the
body lay. Subsequently to the finding
of the body, which had occurred on
Saturday evening, there had been
discovered in a coppice adjoining a
heavy bludgeon-like stick broken in
two. The top of it, which would be
produced, bore the inscription M.
ASSHE . . .

Mr. Taynton was present in court,
and was sitting on the bench to the
right of the judge who had long been
a personal friend of his. Hitherto his
face had been hidden in his hands,

as this terribly logical tale went on.
But here he raised it, and smiled, a
wan smile enough, at Morris. The
latter did not seem to notice the action.
Counsel for the prosecution continued.

All this, he said, had been brought
forward at the trial before the police-
court magistrates, and he thought the
jury would agree that it was more
than sufficient to commit the prisoner
to trial. At that trial, too, they had
heard, the whole world had heard, of
the mystery of the missing watch,
and the missing money. No money,
at least, had been found on the body;
it was reasonable to refer to it as
"missing." But here again, the
motive of self-preservation came in;
the whole thing had been carefully
planned; the prisoner, counsel suggested,
had, just as he had gone up to
town to find Mr. Mills the day
after the murder was committed,
striven to put justice off the scent in

making it appear that the motive for the crime, had been robbery. With well-calculated cunning he had taken the watch and what coins there were, from the pockets of his victim. That at any rate was the theory suggested by the prosecution.

The speech was admirably delivered, and its virtue was its extreme impassiveness; it seemed quite impersonal, the mere automatic action of justice, not revengeful, not seeking for death, but merely stating the case as it might be stated by some planet or remote fixed star. Then there was a short pause, while the prosecutor for the Crown laid down his notes. And the same slow, clear, impassive voice went on.

"But since the committal of the prisoner to stand his trial at these assizes," he said, "more evidence of an utterly unexpected, but to us convincing kind has been discovered. Here it is." And he held up a sheet of blotting paper, and a crumpled envelope.

"A letter has been blotted on this sheet," he said, "and by holding it up to the light and looking through it, one can, of course, read what was written. But before I read it, I will tell you from where this sheet was taken. It was taken from a blotting book in the drawing-room of Mrs. Assheton's house in Sussex Square. An expert in handwriting will soon tell the gentlemen of the jury in whose hand he without doubt considers it to be written. After the committal of the prisoner to trial, search was of course made in this house, for further evidence. This evidence was almost immediately discovered. After that no further search was made."

The judge looked up from his notes.

"By whom was this discovery made?" he asked.

"By Superintendent Figgis and Sergeant Wilkinson, my lord. They will give their evidence."

He waited till the judge had entered this.

"I will read the letter," he said, "from the negative, so to speak, of the blotting paper."

June 21st.

To GODFREY MILLS, Esq.

You damned brute, I will settle you. I hear you are coming back to Brighton to-morrow, and are getting out at Falmer. All right; I shall be there, and we shall have a talk.

MORRIS ASSHETON.

A sort of purr went round the court; the kind humane ladies and gentlemen who had fought for seats found this to their taste. The noose tightened.

"I have here also an envelope," said the prosecutor, "which was found by Mr. Figgis and Mr. Wilkinson in the waste-paper basket in the sitting-

room of the deceased.  According to
the expert in handwriting, whose
evidence you will hear, it is undoubt-
edly addressed by the same hand that
wrote the letter I have just read you.
And, in his opinion, the handwriting
is that of the prisoner.  No letter
was found in the deceased man's room
corresponding to this envelope, but
the jury will observe that what I
have called the negative of the letter
on the blotting-paper was dated June
21st, the day that the prisoner suspected the slander that had been
levelled at him.  The suggestion is
that the deceased opened this before
leaving for London, and took the
letter with him.  And the hand, that
for the purposes of misleading justice,
robbed him of his watch and his
money, also destroyed the letter which
was then on his person, and which
was an incriminating document.  But
this sheet of blotting paper is as

valuable as the letter itself. It proves the letter to have been written."

Morris had been given a seat in the dock, and on each side of him there stood a prison-warder. But in the awed hush that followed, for the vultures and carrion crows who crowded the court were finding themselves quite beautifully thrilled, he wrote a few words on a slip of paper and handed it to a warder to give to his counsel. And his counsel nodded to him.

The opening speech for the Crown had lasted something over two hours, and a couple of witnesses only were called before the interval for lunch. But most of the human ghouls had brought sandwiches with them, and the court was packed with the same people when Morris was brought up again after the interval, and the judge, breathing sherry, took his seat. The

court had become terribly hot, but
the public were too humane to mind
that. A criminal was being chased
toward the gallows, and they followed
his progress there with breathless
interest. Step by step all that was
laid down in the opening speech for
the prosecution was inexorably proved,
all, that is to say, except the affair of
the stick. But from what a certain
witness (Mr. Taynton) swore to, it was
clear that this piece of circumstantial
evidence, which indeed was of the great-
est importance since the Crown's case
was that the murder had been committed with that bludgeon of a stick,
completely broke down. Whoever had
done the murder, he had not done it
with that stick, since Mr. Taynton
deposed to having been at Mrs. Assheton's house on the Friday, the day
after the murder had been committed,
and to having taken the stick away by
mistake, believing it to be his. And

the counsel for the defence only asked
one question on this point, which
question closed the proceedings for
the day. It was:

"You have a similar stick then?"

And Mr. Taynton replied in the
affirmative.

The court then rose.

On the whole the day had been most
satisfactory to the ghouls and vultures
and it seemed probable that they
would have equally exciting and plenti-
ful fare next day. But in the opinion
of many Morris's counsel was dis-
appointing. He did not cross-
examine witnesses at all sensationally,
and drag out dreadful secrets (which
had nothing to do with the case)
about their private lives, in order to
show that they seldom if ever spoke
the truth. Indeed, witness after witness was allowed to escape without any
cross-examination at all; there was no

attempt made to prove that the carpenter who had found the body had been himself tried for murder, or that his children were illegitimate. Yet gradually, as the afternoon went on, a sort of impression began to make its way, that there was something coming which no one suspected.

The next morning those impressions were realised when the adjourned cross-examination of Mr. Taynton was resumed. The counsel for the defence made an immediate attack on the theories of the prosecution, and it told. For the prosecution had suggested that Morris's presence at the scene of the murder the day after was suspicious, as if he had come back uneasily and of an unquiet conscience. If that was so, Mr. Taynton's presence there, who had been the witness who proved the presence of the other, was suspiccious also. What had he come there for? In order to throw the broken

pieces of Morris's stick into the bushes?
These inferences were of course but suggested in the questions counsel asked
Mr. Taynton in the further cross-examination of this morning, and perhaps no
one in court saw what the suggestion
was for a moment or two, so subtly
and covertly was it conveyed. Then
it appeared to strike all minds together,
and a subdued rustle went round the
court, followed the moment after by
an even intenser silence.

Then followed a series of interroga-
tions, which at first seemed wholly
irrelevant, for they appeared to bear
only on the business relations between
the prisoner and the witness. Then
suddenly like the dim light at the end
of a tunnel, where shines the pervading
illuminating sunlight, a little ray
dawned.

"You have had control of the
prisoner's private fortune since 1886?"

"Yes."

"In the year 1896 he had £8,000 or thereabouts in London and North-Western Debentures, £6,000 in Consols, £7,000 in Government bonds of South Australia?"

"I have no doubt those figures are correct."

"A fortnight ago you bought £8,000 of London and North-Western Debentures, £6,000 in Consols, £7,000 in Government bonds of South Australia?"

Mr. Taynton opened his lips to speak, but no sound came from them.

"Please answer the question."

If there had been a dead hush before, succeeding the rustle that had followed the suggestions about the stick, a silence far more palpable now descended. There was no doubt as to what the suggestion was now.

The counsel for the prosecution broke in.

"I submit that these questions are irrelevant, my lord," he said.

"I shall subsequently show, my lord, that they are not."

"The witness must answer the question," said the judge. "I see that there is a possible relevancy."

The question was answered.

"Thank you, that is all," said the counsel for the defence, and Mr. Taynton left the witness box.

It was then, for the first time since the trial began, that Morris looked at this witness. All through he had been perfectly calm and collected, a circumstance which the spectators put down to the callousness with which they kindly credited him, and now for the first time, as Mr. Taynton's eyes and his met, an emotion crossed the prisoner's face. He looked sorry.

# CHAPTER XI

FOR the rest of the morning the examination of witnesses for the prosecution went on, for there were a very large number of them, but when the court rose for lunch, the counsel for the prosecution intimated that this was his last. But again, hardly any but those engaged officially, the judge, the counsel, the prisoner, the warder, left the court. Mr. Taynton, however, went home, for he had his seat on the bench, and he could escape for an hour from this very hot and oppressive atmosphere. But he did not go to his Lewes office, or to any hotel to get his lunch. He went to the station, where after waiting some quarter of an hour, he took the train to Brighton. The train ran through Falmer and from his window he could see where the Park palings made an angle close to the road; it was from there that the path over the Downs, where he had so often walked, passed to Brighton.

Again the judge took his seat, still carrying the little parcel wrapped up in tissue paper.

There was no need for the usher to call silence, for the silence was granted without being asked for.

The counsel for the defence called the first witness; he also unwrapped a flat parcel which he had brought into court with him, and handed it to the witness.

"That was supplied by your firm?"

"Yes sir."

"Who ordered it?"

"Mr. Assheton."

"Mr. Morris Assheton, that is. Did he order it from you, you yourself?"

"Yes, sir."

"Did he give any specific instructions about it?"

"Yes, sir."

"What were they?"

"That the blotting book which Mrs. Assheton had already ordered was to be countermanded, and that this was to be sent in its stead on June 24th."

"You mean not after June 24th?"

"No, sir; the instructions were that it was not to be sent before June 24th."

"Why was that?"

"I could not say, sir. Those were the instructions."

"And it was sent on June 24th."

"Yes, sir. It was entered in our book."

The book in question was produced and handed to the jury and the judge.

"That is all," Mrs. Assheton."

She stepped into the box, and smiled at Morris. There was no murmur of sympathy, no rustling; the whole thing was too tense.

"You returned home on June 24th last, from a visit to town?"

"Yes."

"At what time?"

"I could not say to the minute. But about eleven in the morning.''

"You found letters waiting for you?"

"Yes."

"Anything else?"

"A parcel."

"What did it contain?"

"A blotting-book. It was a present from my son on my birthday."

"Is this the blotting-book?"

"Yes."

"What did you do with it?"

"I opened it and placed it on my writing table in the drawing-room."

"Thank you; that is all."

There was no cross-examination of this witness, and after the pause, the counsel for the defence spoke again.

"Superintendent Figgis."

"You searched the house of Mrs. Assheton in Sussex Square?"

"Yes, sir."

"What did you take from it?"

"A leaf from a blotting-book, sir."

"Was it that leaf which has been already produced in court, bearing the impress of a letter dated June 21st?"

"Yes, sir."

"Where was the blotting-book?"

"On the writing-table in the drawing-room, sir."

"You did not examine the blotting-book in any way?"

"No, sir."

Counsel opened the book and fitted the torn out leaf into its place.

"We have here the impress of a letter dated June 21st, written in a new blotting-book that did not arrive at Mrs. Assheton's house from the shop till June 24th. It threatens — threatens a man who was murdered, supposedly by the prisoner, on June

23d. Yet this threatening letter was not written till June 24th, after he had killed him."

Quiet and unemotional as had been the address for the Crown, these few remarks were even quieter. Then the examination continued.

"You searched also the flat occupied by the deceased, and you found there this envelope, supposedly in the handwriting of the prisoner, which has been produced by the prosecution?"

"Yes, sir."

"This is it?"

"Yes, sir."

"Thank you. That is all."

Again there was no cross-examination, and the superintendent left the witness box.

Then the counsel for the defence took up two blank envelopes in addition to the one already produced and supposedly addressed in the handwriting of the prisoner.

"This blue envelope," he said, "is from the stationery in Mrs. Assheton's house. This other envelope, white, is from the flat of the deceased. It corresponds in every way with the envelope which was supposed to be addressed in the prisoner's hand, found at the flat in question. The inference is that the prisoner blotted the letter dated June 21st on a blotting pad which did not arrive in Mrs. Assheton's house till June 24th, went to the deceased's flat and put it an envelope there.

These were handed to the jury for examination.

"Ernest Smedley," said counsel.

Mills's servant stepped into the box, and was sworn.

"Between, let us say June 21st and June 24th, did the prisoner call at Mr. Mills's flat?"

"Yes, sir, twice."

"When?"

"Once on the evening of June 23d, and once very early next morning."

"Did he go in?"

"Yes, sir, he came in on both occasions."

"What for?"

"To satisfy himself that Mr. Mills had not come back."

"Did he write anything?"

"No, sir."

"How do you know that?"

"I went with him from room to room, and should have seen if he had done so."

"Did anybody else enter the flat during those days?"

"Yes, sir."

"Who?"

"Mr. Taynton."

The whole court seemed to give a great sigh; then it was quiet again. The judge put down the pen with which he had been taking notes, and like the rest of the persons present he only listened.

"When did Mr. Taynton come into the flat?"

"About mid-day or a little later on Friday."

"June 24th?"

"Yes, sir."

"Please tell the jury what he did?"

The counsel for the prosecution stood up.

"I object to that question," he said.

The judge nodded at him; then looked at the witness again. The examination went on.

"You need not answer that question. I put it to save time, merely. Did Mr. Taynton go into the deceased's sitting-room?"

"Yes, sir."

"Did he write anything there?"

"Yes, sir."

"Was he alone there?"

"Yes, sir."

"Thank you."

Again the examining counsel paused,

and again no question was asked by the prosecution.

"Charles Martin," said the counsel for defence.

"You are a servant of the prisoner's?"

"Yes, sir."

"You were in his service during this week of June, of which Friday was June 24th?"

"Yes, sir."

"Describe the events — No. Did the prisoner go up to town, or elsewhere on that day, driving his motorcar, but leaving you in Brighton?"

"Yes, sir."

"Mrs. Assheton came back that morning?"

"Yes, sir."

"Did anyone call that morning? If so, who."

"Mr. Taynton called."

"Did he go to the drawing-room?"

"Yes, sir."

"Did he write anything there?"

"Yes, sir; he wrote a note to Mrs. Assheton, which he gave me when he went out."

"You were not in the drawing-room, when he wrote it?"

"No, sir."

"Did he say anything to you when he left the house?"

"Yes, sir,"

"What did he say?"

The question was not challenged now.

"He told me to say that he had left the note at the door."

"But he had not done so?"

"No, sir; he wrote it in the drawing-room.

"Thank you.  That is all."

But this witness was not allowed to pass as the others had done. The counsel for the prosecution got up.

"You told Mrs. Assheton that it had been left at the door?"

"Yes, sir."

"You knew that was untrue?"

"Yes, sir."

"For what reason did you say it, then?"

Martin hesitated; he looked down, then he looked up again, and was still silent.

"Answer the question."

His eyes met those of the prisoner. Morris smiled at him, and nodded.

"Mr. Taynton told me to say that," he said, "I had once been in Mr. Taynton's service. He dismissed me. I ——"

The judge interposed looking at the cross-examining counsel.

"Do you press your question?" he asked. "I do not forbid you to ask it, but I ask you whether the case for the prosecution of the — the prisoner is furthered by your insisting on this question. We have all heard, the jury and I alike, what the last three or four witnesses have said, and you have allowed that — quite properly, in my opinion — to go unchallenged. I do not myself see that there is anything to be gained by the prosecution by pressing the question. I ask you to consider this point. If you think conscientiously, that the evidence, the trend of which we all know now, is to be shaken, you are right to do your best to try to shake it. If not, I wish you to consider whether you should press the question. What the result of your pressing it will be, I have no idea, but it is certainly clear to us all now, that there was a threat implied in Mr. Taynton's words. Personally I do not wish to know what that threat was, nor do I see how the knowledge of it would affect your case in my eyes, or in the eyes of the jury."

There was a moment's pause.

"No, my lord, I do not press it."

Then a clear young voice broke the silence.

"Thanks, Martin," it said.

It came from the dock.

The judge looked across to the dock for a moment, with a sudden irresistible impulse of kindliness for the prisoner whom he was judging.

"Charles Martin," he said, "you have given your evidence, and speaking for myself, I believe it to be entirely trustworthy. I wish to say that your character is perfectly clear. No aspersion whatever has been made on it, except that you said a note had been delivered at the door, though you knew it to have been not so delivered. You made that statement through fear of a certain individual; you were frightened into telling a lie. No one inquires into the sources of your fear."

But in the general stillness, there was one part of the court that was not still, but the judge made no command of silence there, for in the jury-box there was whispering and consultation.

It went on for some three minutes. Then the foreman of the jury stood up.

"The jury have heard sufficient of this case, my lord," he said, "and they are agreed on their verdict."

For a moment the buzzing whispers went about the court again, shrilling high, but instantaneously they died down, and the same tense silence prevailed. But from the back of the court there was a stir, and the judge seeing what it was that caused it waited, while Mrs. Assheton moved from her place, and made her way to the front of the dock in which Morris sat. She had been in the witness-box that day, and everyone knew her, and all made way for her, moving as the blades of corn move when the wind stirs them, for her right was recognised and unquestioned. But the dock was high above her, and a barrister who sat below instantly vacated his seat, she got up and stood on it.  All eyes were fixed on her, and none saw that at this moment a telegram was handed to the judge which he opened and read.

Then he turned to the foreman of the jury.

"What verdict, do you find?" he asked.

"Not guilty."

Mrs. Assheton had already grasped Morris's hands in hers, and just as the words were spoken she kissed him.

Then a shout arose which bade fair to lift the roof off, and neither judge nor ushers of the court made any attempt to quiet it, and if it was only for the sensation of seeing the gallows march nearer the prisoner that these folk had come together, yet there was no mistaking the genuineness of their congratulations now.  Morris's whole behaviour too, had been so gallant and brave; innocent though he knew himself to be, yet it required a very high courage to listen to the damning accumulation of evidence against him, and if there is one thing that the ordinary man appreciates more than sensation, it is pluck. Then, but not for a long time, the uproar subsided, and the silence descended again. Then the judge spoke.

"Mr. Assheton," he said, "for I no longer can call you prisoner, the jury have of course found you not guilty of the terrible crime of which you were accused, and I need not say that I entirely agree with their verdict. Throughout the trial you have had my sympathy and my admiration for your gallant bearing." Then at a sign from the judge his mother and he were let out by the private door below the bench.

After they had gone silence was restored. Everyone knew that there must be more to come. The prisoner was found not guilty; the murder was still unavenged.

Then once more the judge spoke.

"I wish to make public recognition," he said, "of the fairness and ability with which the case was conducted on both sides. The prosecution, as it was their duty to do, forged the chain of evidence against Mr. Assheton as strongly as they were able, and pieced together incriminating circumstances against him with a skill that at first seemed conclusive of his guilt. The first thing that occured to make a weak link in their chain was the acknowledgment of a certain witness that the stick with which the murder was supposed to have been committed was not left on the spot by the accused, but by himself. Why he admitted that we can only conjecture, but my conjecture is that it was an act of repentance and contrition on his part. When it came to that point he could not let the evidence which he had himself supplied tell against him on whom it was clearly his object to father the crime. You will remember also that certain circumstances pointed to robbery being the motive of the crime. That I think was the first idea, so to speak of the real criminal. Then, we must suppose, he saw himself safer, if he forged against another certain evidence which we have heard."

The judge paused for a moment, and then went on with evident emotion.

"This case will never be reöpened again," he said, "for a reason that I will subsequently tell the court; we have seen the last of this tragedy, and retribution and punishment are in the hands of a higher and supreme tribunal. This witness, Mr. Edward Taynton — has been for years a friend of mine, and the sympathy which I felt for him at the opening of the case, when a young man, to whom I still believe him to have been attached, was on his trial, is changed to a deeper pity. During the afternoon you have heard certain evidence, from which you no doubt as well as I infer that the fact of this murder having been committed was known to the man who wrote a letter and blotted it on the sheet which has been before the court. That man also, as it was clear to us an hour ago, directed a certain envelope which you have also seen. I may add that Mr. Taynton had, as I knew, an extraordinary knack of imitating handwritings; I have seen him write a signature that I could have sworn was mine. But he has used that gift for tragic purposes.

I have just received a telegram. He left this court before the luncheon interval, and went to his house in Brighton. Arrived there, as I have just learned, he poisoned himself. And may God have mercy on his soul."

Again he paused.

"The case therefore is closed," he said, "and the court will rise for the day. You will please go out in silence."

## THE HOGARTH PRESS

This is a paperback list for today's readers – but it holds to a tradition of adventurous and original publishing set by Leonard and Virginia Woolf when they founded The Hogarth Press in 1917 and started their first paperback series in 1924.

Some of the books are light-hearted, some serious, and include Fiction, Lives and Letters, Travel, Critics, Poetry, History and Hogarth Crime and Gaslight Crime.

A list of our books already published, together with some of our forthcoming titles, follows. If you would like more information about Hogarth Press books, write to us for a catalogue:

30 Bedford Square, London WC1B 3RP

*Please send a large stamped addressed envelope*

# HOGARTH FICTION

# E. F. Benson
## *The Freaks of Mayfair*

New Introduction by Christopher Hawtree

Impaled on the pin of Benson's genius are prime specimens of Edwardian society: inveterate snobs and vicious gossips rolling up to receptions in Belgravia; young men with a taste for embroidery; health-cult devotees playing badminton in parquetted ballrooms; fossilised dowagers off to séances in Chesterfield Square. Here, in a fictional extravaganza, illustrated with the marvellous original line-drawings, are the bizarre, the great and the good E. F. Benson knew so well and all the forerunners of the unforgettable characters in his novels.

# E. F. Benson
## *The Luck of the Vails*
### New Introduction by Stephen Knight

E. F. Benson is best known for his hilarious novels and delightful memoirs, but he was also a grand teller of evil tales. Set amid the rolling Wiltshire dales and the clattering gaslit streets of London, *The Luck of the Vails* reveals a long history of corruption and violence amongst the old aristocracy. It is a vintage crime story.

# Fergus Hume
## *Madame Midas*

### New Introduction by Stephen Knight

Madame Midas is a woman who knows her own mind, but not her own heart. Charming, of humble origins, she stakes her claim in a land of pioneers and soon returns to Melbourne laden with gold. But the streets of that city are paved with envy, betrayal, cruelty and crime. Slowly but surely, Madame Midas hardens to the touch.

Sought after for years, *Madame Midas* is now republished for the first time since original publication – bringing to an end a century of notorious neglect. It is a rivetting salutory story and, like *Hansom Cab*, a sharply realistic picture of Victorian times – a nugget of pure gold.

# Margery Allingham
## *Cargo of Eagles*

Two roads lead to Saltey, an ancient hamlet on the Essex estuary: one is fast, frequented by mods and rockers on holiday weekends; the other is a dirt track, almost hidden by centuries of misuse by black-hearted smugglers. But, as Albert Campion learns in this masterly crime story, few roads lead out. For Saltey holds a secret rich and enigmatic enough to trap all who enter, despite someone's best endeavours to terrorize, murder and raise the very devil to keep that secret to themselves.